They heard her unlock the door, and instantly Tim threw his weight against it. Jessica yelped once as she was thrown down. Then Tim was on her, with Robby close behind, a short length of rope in his hands. Instantly he twisted the rope about her ankles and knotted it . . . then she shoved him away with both feet and he slammed against the wall, seeing stars and bright lights for a moment.

Tim was trying to hold her down, but she wrestled him, hitting his arm with a painful blow. He growled, rolling away. She tried to get to her feet and fell.

Tim swore at Robby. "Where the hell are you?"

Robby crawled to the woman, grabbing at her arms. He took a fist in the face and tasted blood before he captured one arm. Tim had the other, and between them they managed to get a rope around her wrists.

Realizing they had her tied, Jessica took a breath to yell, and Robby crammed a wad of cloth in her mouth. She struggled, but he knotted another cloth about her head to hold it . . .

Also in the LONE STAR series from Jove

LONGARM AND THE LONE STAR LEGEND
LONE STAR AND THE MOUNTAIN MAN
LONE STAR AND THE STOCKYARD SHOWDOWN
LONE STAR AND THE RIVERBOAT GAMBLERS
LONE STAR AND THE MESCALERO OUTLAWS
LONE STAR AND THE AMARILLO RIFLES
LONE STAR AND THE SCHOOL FOR OUTLAWS
LONE STAR ON THE TREASURE RIVER
LONE STAR AND THE MOON TRAIL FEUD
LONE STAR AND THE GOLDEN MESA
LONE STAR AND THE RIO GRANDE BANDITS
LONE STAR AND THE BUFFALO HUNTERS
LONE STAR AND THE BIGGEST GUN IN THE WEST
LONE STAR AND THE APACHE WARRIOR
LONE STAR AND THE GOLD MINE WAR
LONE STAR AND THE CALIFORNIA OIL WAR
LONE STAR AND THE ALASKAN GUNS
LONE STAR AND THE WHITE RIVER CURSE
LONE STAR AND THE TOMBSTONE GAMBLE
LONE STAR AND THE TIMBERLAND TERROR
LONE STAR IN THE CHEROKEE STRIP
LONE STAR AND THE OREGON RAIL SABOTAGE
LONE STAR AND THE MISSION WAR
LONE STAR AND THE LAND BARONS
LONE STAR AND THE GULF PIRATES
LONE STAR AND THE INDIAN REBELLION
LONE STAR AND THE NEVADA MUSTANGS
LONE STAR AND THE CON MAN'S RANSOM
LONE STAR AND THE STAGECOACH WAR
LONE STAR AND THE TWO GUN KID
LONE STAR AND THE SIERRA SWINDLERS
LONE STAR IN THE BIG HORN MOUNTAINS
LONE STAR AND THE DEATH TRAIN
LONE STAR AND THE RUSTLER'S AMBUSH
LONE STAR AND THE TONG'S REVENGE
LONE STAR AND THE OUTLAW POSSE
LONE STAR AND THE SKY WARRIORS
LONE STAR IN A RANGE WAR
LONE STAR AND THE PHANTOM GUNMEN
LONE STAR AND THE MONTANA LAND GRAB
LONE STAR AND THE JAMES GANG'S LOOT
LONE STAR AND THE MASTER OF DEATH
LONE STAR AND THE CHEYENNE TRACKDOWN
LONE STAR AND THE LOST GOLD MINE
LONE STAR AND THE COMANCHEROS
LONE STAR AND HICKOK'S GHOST
LONE STAR AND THE DEADLY STRANGER

WESLEY ELLIS

LONE STAR AND THE SILVER BANDITS

J

JOVE BOOKS, NEW YORK

LONE STAR AND THE SILVER BANDITS

A Jove Book / published by arrangement with
the author

PRINTING HISTORY
Jove edition / August 1988

ISBN: 0-515-09683-0

Jove Books are published by The Berkley Publishing Group,
200 Madison Avenue, New York, New York 10016.
The name "JOVE" and the "J" logo
are trademarks belonging to Jove Publications, Inc.

PRINTED IN THE UNITED STATES OF AMERICA

10 9 8 7 6 5 4 3 2 1

Chapter 1

Jessica Starbuck watched the rider come across the weedy field toward the house. As he came closer she recognized him as old Johnny Hinkle, a man who did odd jobs for several of the merchants in town. She waved as he approached, and when he got down at the hitchrail she rose and walked out to meet him.

"Hello, Johnny. What brings you out this way?"

"Got a letter f'you, Miss Jessie." He felt inside his brown vest. He was an old-timer with a weathered face and clawlike hands. He brought out the letter and handed it over with a flourish. "Sam, at the post office, he figured you'd want it right off, like. Might be important, he said."

"Hummm." She looked at the signature. It was written in a clear, bold hand. She didn't recognize the writing or the return name on the back. Homer Wills. Who was Homer Wills?

She smiled at Johnny. "Come on in for a cup of coffee. We've got some venison left . . ."

"No thanks, Miss Jessie. Sam tole me t'get on back. He got some sheds he wants cleared out. But thankee just the same." He untied the reins and stepped up, settling himself in the saddle. He tipped his hat and turned the horse.

Jessie walked back to the porch, tearing open the envelope. There was a single sheet of paper inside.

> Dear Miss Starbuck:
> Something's happened to your friend Vance Collworth in Eagle Rock. Come and see for yourself.
> There ain't any Homer Wills. I made it up.
> A friend.

That was all. Just a few bare lines. And signed "A friend." That could be anyone. She frowned at the paper. It was a sheet torn from a tablet; it had faint blue lines and was of cheap quality. She folded it back into the envelope and tapped it against her chin. Ki was away on some chore or other and wouldn't be back until dark.

Vance Collworth. She hadn't thought of him for years. She had met him when she'd been about twelve, maybe fourteen. Vance and Jessie's father, Alex, had been close. Vance had helped her father out of a particular jam in the old days and they'd been friends ever since. As a matter of fact, she had a tintype of Vance and her father together in a studio, a picture taken in front of a Rocky Mountain backdrop. It had stood on a sideboard for years. Vance had been a lawman when the picture had been taken. He was a straight-shooting, handsome man with a black mustache . . . the mustache was probably gray by now.

What was he doing in Eagle Rock? Was he still a lawman? She shook her head in annoyance. Her "friend" should have told her more in the letter.

She showed Ki the letter when he arrived after dark. He read it and asked who Vance Collworth was, so she explained.

". . . I ought to go to Eagle Rock and see—"

"That's a long ride, you know." Ki fingered the letter. "It could be from a crank. I don't care for unsigned letters."

Jessie nodded. "But just the same, I'm curious. How would this person know that I know Vance?"

Ki shrugged. "Well, when you make up your mind, you make up your mind. I suppose we ought to start packing."

She laughed. "Yes, we may as well."

Ki found a map that had been printed by a stagecoach company and they pored over it, deciding on a route. Eagle Rock was a smallish town in the mountains, well away from other towns, with only a single road through it. There were silver mines in the vicinity that were still working, so the town probably enjoyed a good payroll each month. And there were cattle ranches nearby also, and probably cowboys shooting at the moon now and again, as they left the town's various saloons and staggered out to their mounts.

Ki and Jessie were old hands at packing and traveling, and after a few hours they were on the trail. They followed a post road for a few dozen miles, then cut across country, guided by Ki's compass and the stars.

They saw deer and even a few distant wolves, but no humans until they came across unexpected and tiny settlements. They spent several nights under roofs, but mostly they slept under the glittering stars. The weather was fair and the miles dropped away behind them. In five days they saw the foothills ahead, and the next day they were in the long valley that led to Eagle Rock.

It was dusk when they sighted the town, the lights winking in the distance. A ground fog had risen, slightly clammy, smoothing the ridges on either side. The buildings had an old, settled look to them; it was not a new town, and not a large one: just a main street crossed by several small side streets.

It was apparently a quiet night. There were a few wagons on the street and perhaps twenty horses at hitchrails here and there. Music came from the well-lighted saloons and a few men were walking along the street or standing in groups, talking. No one seemed to pay them any attention when they got down in front of the hotel and went inside.

It was called the Granger House. There was a fading sign behind the desk: CASH ONLY. G. R. GRANGER, PROP.

The small, square lobby room smelled of dust. The man behind the desk was skinny and bald with steel-rimmed glasses that made his eyes round. He gave them a professional smile. "You just ride in?"

"Just this minute," Jessie said. "We'd like two rooms, please."

"You ain't together then?"

“We’re together, but we’re not,” Ki told him. “Have you got two rooms?”

“Oh yes, sure.” He turned the dog-eared ledger around and scratched at the nib of a pen with his finger to get dried ink off it. He gave the pen to Jessie and pushed an ink bottle toward her.

She signed her name and Ki signed under hers. The clerk turned the ledger and read the names. “Welcome to Eagle Rock. My name’s Kinch, you want anything. I don’t think there’s any restaurant open yet tonight . . .”

“We’ll make do,” Ki said. “Thanks.” He took their keys as Kinch said, “Rooms 10 and 11. Upstairs.”

Jessie went up first, and met two men at the top. They were rough looking, dressed in wool shirts, with their pants tucked into high boots. One of them, who had a beard, grabbed Jessie and pulled her into his arms, laughing. The other slapped her buttocks.

She yelled in surprise and flailed her arms. Her elbow slammed into the bearded one’s cheek and he howled in pain. As the man drew back his fist, Ki kicked his knee and he fell forward, nearly spilling down the steps. The second man drew a pistol and Ki kicked it away. Jessie pushed him and Ki pulled him by the arm and he tumbled down the stairs to land in a heap at the bottom.

The beard got up slowly, his eyes showing rage. “Why you stinkin’ little Chinee—” He slid a long knife from his belt and sliced at Ki with it. Ki ducked away and the man charged. Ki fell back and his feet propelled the big man over his head. The bearded one landed heavily. Ki danced close and kicked the knife away from him. Jessie picked it and the pistol up.

The big man was shaking his head to clear it. Ki grabbed his foot and dragged him to the head of the stairs. At the last minute the man realized what was happening, and he tried to lunge at Ki. But Ki slid around him and shoved out with one foot, and the bearded man fell down the stairs to land atop his companion.

Ki grinned at Jessie. “Welcome to Eagle Rock.”

Chapter 2

The rest of the night passed uneventfully. Jessie and Ki were both up early, and they met in the little lobby downstairs. Kinch was gone, and in his place was an older man, partly deaf and half asleep. His name was George, he told them, and the best place for breakfast was Harry's Restaurant, just along the street a few doors.

Jessie asked him, "Do you know Vance Collworth?"

"Sure, ma'am. Ever'body knows him. He runs the Golden Slipper."

"He's not a lawman?"

George shook his head. "Naw. We got Ned Hilton f'that. He's the town marshal. Vance was the marshal, but he give the job to Ned."

"Is Mr. Collworth all right?" Jessie persisted.

"I guess so." George shrugged. "I don't go up to th' Slipper, ma'am. I ain't a gamblin' man m'self." He gave them a wan smile. "Ain't got the money t'lose."

"What kind of a town is it?" Ki asked.

"Busy," George said. "Ever'body diggin' silver, or haulin' it."

Ki looked out at the street. "Seems peaceful enough."

"Oh, that's because it's only Thursday. And besides, all the men's workin' in the mines." George waved his pudgy hands. "These here hills is fulla mines. You wait: come Saturday night the town'll be jumpin'. Cowboys comes in too. They-all has theirselves a holler, I tell you."

"Can we find Mr. Collworth at the Slipper, then?"

George shrugged. "I really couldn't say. Him'n me, we don't pull at the same towel."

Jessie thanked him and they went out and up the street to the restaurant. Harry's place was a long, narrow room with a few tables in the back. There was a black-haired woman behind the counter, wiping glasses. She stared at the newcomer with the honey-blond hair and sea-green eyes, almost dropping her mouth open. The cook came from the kitchen to stand in the doorway, round-eyed.

Jessie nodded to each of them and took a table, ignoring the men at the counter stools who craned their necks at her. Ki sat opposite and picked up a menu. His back was to the door, to the men at the counter; he did not turn as Jessie drew a pistol and laid it on the table in front of her, covering it with her menu.

She said softly, "One of the men you tossed down the steps last night is at the counter."

"Is he getting up?"

"I think he's making up his mind about something. He's growling to himself."

"When he moves he may do it fast."

She slid her hand over the pistol grip. "He's getting up now."

Ki nodded. His hand slid inside his vest, fingers closing over a *shuriken*. He kept his eyes on Jessie's. When he saw them widen, he threw himself sideways, the throwing star in his hand as he darted a glance back— But there was no need to throw it. He saw the bearded man rushing toward them, a pistol raised, but Jessie's three shots blasted him in the neck and chest and hurled him backward. The pistol went flying and he crumpled to the hard floor as the sounds of the shots re-echoed in the little room, mauling their ears.

For a moment there was a deathly silence. Then the chatter

rose like a wave, with everyone talking at once. Jessie was standing, the six-gun in her hand, and they stared at her as she slowly punched out the used brass and reloaded.

Ki knelt over the fallen man, feeling for a pulse, and shook his head.

The owner, Harry, came awake and demanded that some of them haul the body out to the sidewalk. "You, Jerry, you go fer the law, and tell Mr. Nick they's a body here f'him."

A younger man nodded and went out at once.

Harry looked at Jessica. "What'd you want to shoot 'im for, miss?"

She made a face. "He was going to shoot me." She sat down, looking at the menu. "I'll have two eggs over easy, with bacon."

Harry nodded. "Comin' up." He went back into the kitchen.

The town law, Ned Hilton, was more curious than Harry had been. He asked them to his office, a square stone building with the jail attached, and asked them questions, writing down their answers carefully.

"You never seen this man before—is that so?"

"Never." Jessica gave him a rundown on the two they had met at the top of the stairs the night before. Hilton nodded, his pen busy.

"You don't know their names?"

Jessie shook her head. "Certainly not."

Ned said, "The man you shot is—I guess I should say *was*, Fred Hickson. The other one is his brother, Tim Hickson. He's got a broken arm." He looked at Ki curiously. "You knocked them both downstairs?"

"It was necessary," Ki said gently.

"Um-hum. Well, he's only got one arm for a while now, but he's dangerous. I'd watch my backtrail if I was you."

"Is he a miner?" Jessie asked.

Ned shook his head. "He works for Vance Collworth at the Slipper." He looked at them quizzically. "You two just passin' through?"

"No," Jessie said. "We plan to stay for a bit." She smiled at him. "Are you holding us?"

"No, ma'am. They was plenty of witnesses that he was tryin' to shoot you." He put the pen down and folded the writing paper.

Jessie stood. "Thank you then, Mr. Hilton." She went out, followed by Ki. They walked away from the building slowly. "None of this sounds like Vance Collworth," she said.

"What do you mean?"

"I mean that Collworth was always a lawman. I was only a girl when I knew him, but I can't imagine him owning a saloon. And he certainly wouldn't hire a man like Hickson."

"People change," Ki said.

She sighed. "Not that much. Let's go calling on Mr. Collworth."

"Will he remember you?"

"Maybe not. But he'll remember my father." She glanced at the sky. "All I'll have to do is mention his name."

Chapter 3

The Golden Slipper was the largest saloon and dance hall in town, twice as large as its nearest competitor. And it was in the center of town, impossible to miss. It was open twenty-four hours a day, according to the sign out front.

It was ten in the morning when they went inside. The place was nearly deserted. The dance-hall was closed; the large doors between it and the saloon were drawn, and little signs said OPEN AT 5 PM.

The main saloon room was large. There was a grand bar on the left, with mirrors behind it, and shining pyramids of glassware. Two small boys were sitting on the floor polishing brass. No one stood at the bar, but three men were playing cards at one of the many tables. They turned to stare at the woman who had walked into the province of men.

Jessie stood looking at the elegant room. There was a large stage at the back; the footlights were not lit and the curtain was down, but it was the best stage she'd seen outside of Kansas City. There was probably another one in the dance-hall.

One of the men at the table said, "You-all want something?"

Jessie said, "I'm looking for Vance Collworth."

"He's upstairs, sleeping," the man said. "Come back t'night."

"When will he come down?"

The man made a face and lifted a shoulder. "Maybe around nine this evening. Can't tell about Vance. What you want him for?"

"He's an old friend."

"That so? Didn't know he knew any folks around here."

Jessica smiled. "I'm not from around here."

The man nodded. "I'll tell 'im."

Outside on the street she said, "Something isn't right. I can feel it in my bones."

"Because he sleeps late? He's probably up all night in the saloon."

"I suppose so . . ."

"We ought to find out more about this town. Why don't we go back and talk to the marshal again?"

Jessica nodded. "That's a good idea."

They retraced their steps, but when they went inside the stone building, the marshal was absent. Instead a younger man greeted them pleasantly. "Hello. I'm Deputy Marshal Jack English. The marshal was called out. Anything I can do for you?" His gaze lingered on Jessica.

She smiled and introduced Ki. The two men shook hands. English said, "So you know Vance Collworth?"

Jessie said, "I haven't seen him for many years. He may not recognize me. . . . He and my father were friends." She and Ki sat in the heavy wooden chairs before the desk.

The deputy leaned his elbows on the desk pad. "Collworth's the biggest man in these parts, you know. Well, the biggest in town, anyway."

Ki said, "You mean the richest?"

English smiled. "I mean the most powerful. You cross Mr. Collworth and you may as well leave town."

Jessie thought that was an unusual thing for a lawman to say, but maybe Jack English was an unusual lawman. He was certainly a good-looking young man, about her own age. He looked well able to take care of himself.

Ki asked, "How long has he been here in Eagle Rock?"

"I don't know. He was here when I came. I've only seen him a few times, matter of fact. He doesn't circulate much."

Jessie said, "They told us at the saloon that he comes down about nine o'clock."

"Yes, but then he stays in his office or in one of the back rooms. You seldom see him in the saloon. Do you have something to see him about?"

Jessie shrugged. "Only that he and my father were close. He was like family when I was a girl."

"I see."

Ki asked, "Is Collworth interested in cattle or mining?"

"Mining. I'm told he has interests in several mines. I don't think he cares a bit about cattle." English smiled again. "I'm only relating the local gossip, of course. Collworth doesn't take me into his confidence."

"He used to be interested in cattle," Jessie said musingly. "He certainly has changed."

"Tell us about the town itself," Ki asked.

"It's a town," English said guardedly. He gave a little shrug. "It's a tough town . . ."

"I see no churches or schools," Jessie offered.

"There aren't any. You want to go to church, it's a forty mile ride. I don't think there're any kids here at all. Every woman in town works in one of the saloons or dance-halls." English ran a hand through his dark hair. "When the miners come into town"—he shook his head—"we fill up the jail."

"Is it a well run town?" Ki asked.

English looked at him for a moment. "No."

"Who runs it?"

"Vance Collworth." English reached into his shirt pocket and pulled out the makin's. He began to roll a brown cigarette. Jessie and Ki exchanged glances.

Jessie said, "This doesn't sound like Vance Collworth at all. Is there someone else in charge, using his name?"

English shook his head. He licked the edge of the paper and formed the cigarette carefully. He said very softly, "He has a gang around him, yes. But he makes the decisions."

"A gang?" She was surprised.

"Yes." English struck a match and blew smoke. "There are half a dozen around him. His second in command is Harry Pike. They call him 'Nails.' He's a gunman, and pretty good."

"Thank you for telling us this," Jessie said.

English smiled. "Well, I've heard of you two. You have some sort of rep, you know. The reports are, you're on the side of law and order."

"That's true," Jessie acknowledged. "What about the marshal?"

"I've told you about all I can." English got up from behind the desk.

"What about the cattlemen?" Ki persisted. "Are they behind Collworth or against him?"

"There's no love lost between them," English said. "Collworth is close to *some* of the miners, as I said . . . but not all. The cattlemen's organization is led by a man named Jonas Clark. I know very little about him."

"Thank you again," Jessie said.

She talked very briefly to the grocer in the general store. She asked him what Vance Collworth looked like, and he told her the man was stocky, with glasses, not a great deal of hair, and a very definite way of speaking.

This was as she remembered Collworth—though of course he'd had more hair when he was younger. What had changed him so much?

"I'll go to the saloon tonight," she told Ki, "and try to see him."

"You can't go in there!"

"Why not?"

"Because this isn't an ordinary town—and they don't like women in saloons in those towns either—but this one is worse. You heard the deputy say all the women in town worked in the saloons or dance-halls. What kind of work do you suppose they do?"

"But how will I see Mr. Collworth, then?"

"I don't know, but you can't just wander into the saloon. I'll go instead."

"But you don't know Vance."

“Someone will point him out. I’ll ask him to meet you at the hotel.”

She sighed. “Very well. I guess that’ll have to do, like it or not. But I don’t like you going in there alone.”

Ki shrugged. “You said he’s a friend of yours.”

“He *was* my father’s friend. But from what I’ve heard recently—”

“We’ll know more tonight after I see him.”

She sighed again. “I wonder why it worries me so much . . .”

Chapter 4

The street had no lights at all; the only illumination came from the few open stores and the saloons. A few shadowy figures moved along the boardwalks as Ki approached the Golden Slipper. A man sat at the edge of the street singing softly to himself, a bottle in his hand. From somewhere off down the street a dog barked furiously, and from another direction came the sounds of several shots.

Ki paused, listening. His fingers crept into his vest and he touched the *shuriken* hidden there. To the casual observer, he was unarmed. No one he could see paid any apparent attention to the shots. Maybe that sort of thing was common after dark. He thought of Jack English's statement that Eagle Rock was a tough town.

He had been in tough towns before. Some of the worst were rotten from the top down; was that the case here? Jack English had seemed an honest man—but was his boss, Ned Hilton? And was Vance Collworth? Ki shook his head. He didn't know.

Three men on horseback came galloping along the street toward him, and Ki paused. All three began shooting into the air and yelling. They got down in front of a saloon and went inside, talking loudly. Three cowhands out for fun... announcing their arrival.

He pushed open the swinging doors of the Slipper and stepped inside. It was quite different from the room he'd seen earlier. Now it was ablaze with lights, and though it was only a weeknight, it was busy with men—and painted girls. He pulled the hat lower over his face and moved into the room, heading for the long bar.

A few musicians were tuning up near the stage. Ki saw there was a piano there now, just below the footlights. The stage curtain was different too. Apparently a show was about to begin. He reached the bar and put his foot on the brass rail. A bartender approached, dressed in white shirt and red tie, and Ki said, "Beer."

The bartender nodded and drew a stein, sliding it in front of Ki, his other hand capturing the coin Ki put on the bar. He was about to turn away, but then he leaned toward Ki.

"What're you, a chink?"

Ki shook his head. "Part Japanese."

A man next to him said, "Same goddamn thing."

Ki glanced at him. "Not quite."

The man said loudly to the bartender, "You started serving chinks in here, Bo?"

The room became a little more quiet. Ki felt everyone was staring at him. He sipped the beer casually. "My money's good."

"Well, what about it?" the man demanded. "You servin' these slant-eyes or not?"

Ki tossed the rest of the beer in the man's face.

He was a burly man and he roared in rage, his eyes suddenly wild. He grabbed at his pistol, and as it cleared the holster Ki kicked out. The gun went flying and Ki hit him alongside the head with the heavy glass stein. The man dropped to the floor, sprawling.

Ki said, "Another beer, please." He put a coin on the bar.

Instantly men were chattering again. Some laughed, and two came from the crowd and poured water on the unconscious man, who came awake dazedly. Ki drank the beer and watched them carry him outside. Someone laid the pistol on the bar and the bartender dropped it on a shelf under the bar.

Then a lanky, smiling man was suddenly beside him. "Care t'tell me your name, friend?"

"Ki." He looked the man over: fancy vest over a starched white shirt, and a blue bow tie. He wore pressed pants with a silver buckle on the belt. If he were armed it didn't show. Maybe there was a derringer under the vest.

"You just passin' through, are you?"

Ki said, "I came to see Mr. Collworth." *This man must be Nails. . . .* "I imagine you're Mr. Pike."

"That's right. What's your business with Vance?"

"I came to ask him to meet an old friend." Ki was suddenly aware that two large men had moved up behind him. The room was very quiet now.

"An old friend?"

"Yes, from some years ago."

"I see," Nails said in an even tone. "How does it happen that you're here instead of the old friend?"

Ki smiled. "Because it's a woman."

Nails nodded. He indicated the door. "Shall we go outside for a little air."

It wasn't a question. Ki turned, and the four of them moved to the door and outside to the boardwalk. Nails rolled a thin black cigar in his fingers and his tone continued, low and even. "Mr. Collworth isn't interested in seeing old friends. I suggest you take the woman to the stage depot and both of you move along."

"He won't see her?"

"No, he won't. You be on the stage in the morning." Nails nodded pleasantly and went back inside. His two henchmen followed.

Ki looked after them in surprise. He wouldn't see Jessie? He didn't even ask who the "friend" was. That was damned curious.

He headed back to the hotel. Jessica wasn't going to like any of this.

Tim Hickson eased his broken arm, wincing as a stab of pain shot up to his shoulder. The doc had splinted it and put it in a neck bandage, but when he moved the wrong way it hurt. All because of that damned Chinee in the saloon.

And the honey-blond girl.

He rubbed a hand over his stubbled jaw, thinking of her. There wasn't a single girl in any of the saloons or dance-halls in town who could hold a candle to her. Not one.

He looked along the street. Robby should be here by now. It was almost ten o'clock. He drew back into the shadows, watching the door of the hotel across the street. No one had gone in or out for a half-hour. The girl had to be in her room —where would she go?

He stepped out onto the boards as a horseman approached. It was Robby, on a sorrel horse. He leaned down as Tim spoke: "Go around back in the alley behind the hotel. I'll meet you there."

"Yeh," Robby said. He moved away.

Tim watched until the other had disappeared in the gloom. Then, glancing around carefully, he crossed the street and entered a narrow passageway that led to the alley between two buildings.

It was darker here, and much quieter; the noises from the several saloons did not reach except for an occasional yell. The alleyway was deeply rutted from wagons and hoofs. It was used to go to and from stables, and for deliveries to stores. It was also lined with privies and sheds. Tim leaned against one and waited till Robby materialized, walking the sorrel. He got down and tied the animal next to Tim's roan horse.

"What we goin' do?" Robby asked, gazing at the dark mass of the hotel. He rubbed his big hands on his jeans.

"Wait'll you see this gal. You'll know what t'do."

"Ain't she liable to scream?" Robby was skinny and a little stooped though he was only thirty. He had squinty eyes and very little chin. He and Tim had known each other for years . . . hit a lot of whorehouses together.

"We'll tie her goddamn mouth," Tim said. "C'mon, let's git at it." He went up the steps to the back door. When he pulled it open it squeaked. He stepped inside. Robby came in behind him.

"Where is she?"

"Upstairs."

"How you know?"

"Why the hell you figger we're here?" Tim growled. "I heard Orville tellin' some bird in the rest'rant about her. That's how." Orville was a hotel clerk. "He said she's in room 10."

It was dark in the hallway. The only lantern lit was in the tiny lobby fifty feet away, and its feeble glow did not reach the hall . . . or the stairs. However, there was a small lantern hanging from a wire at the top of the steps.

Room 10 was three doors down. Tim struck a match to make sure of the number painted on the door in black. Then he looked at Robby and scratched on the door. "When she opens it, go in quick."

Robby nodded.

Tim scratched again and they could hear someone moving inside. A woman's voice said, "That you, Ki?"

"Yes . . ." Tim said softly. He touched the door with his shoulder.

They heard her unlock the door, and instantly Tim threw his weight against it. The woman yelped once as she was thrown down. Then Tim was on her, with Robby close behind, a short length of rope in his hands. Instantly he twisted the rope about her ankles and knotted it . . . then she shoved him away with both feet and he slammed against the wall, seeing stars and bright lights for a moment.

Tim was trying to hold her down, but she wrestled him, hitting his arm with a painful blow. He growled, rolling away. She tried to get to her feet and fell.

Tim swore at Robby. "Where the hell are you?"

Robby crawled to the woman, grabbing at her arms. He took a fist in the face and tasted blood before he captured one arm. Tim had the other, and between them they managed to get a rope around her wrists.

Realizing they had her tied, Jessica took a breath to yell, and Robby crammed a wad of cloth in her mouth. She struggled, but he knotted another cloth about her head to hold it.

Then they picked her up and headed for the door.

Chapter 5

Ki walked slowly back to the hotel, thinking over what he'd seen and heard. Was Nails able to speak for Collworth in that manner? Collworth didn't want to see anyone—no matter who? Did that make sense?

He stood for a time, leaning against a building, looking at the dark street. Someone was pounding a piano in the nearest saloon while a chorus of unlikely voices accompanied it.

He and Jessie were to leave town by the next day? Very high-handed. He glanced around as several shots sounded, half a block away, and he heard glass shatter. Yes, it was a tough town. He didn't envy Jack English his job.

But the undertaker, whoever he was, was doubtless socking money away. It probably cost fifteen or twenty dollars to bury a man these days. Not counting the gravestone.

Shaking his head, he went inside the hotel and paused by the desk. The clerk was asleep in an easy chair, snoring gently.

Ki went up the stairs, wondering how Jessie would take what he had to tell her. She definitely would not like it.

He paused by her door and thought about knocking. But

she was probably asleep. . . . He could tell her in the morning.

Then he noticed the door was ajar. It was open only about an inch, and in the gloom of the hall he hadn't seen it at once. He pushed the door open. A lantern was lit by the bed, and as his gaze took in the room he saw a chair overturned.

Jessie was not in the room.

The window was closed tight. Nothing else was disturbed that he could see. He righted the chair with an icy hand gripping his heart. Some person or persons had come into the room and managed to take her away—and they would have their hands full. Had they killed her?

He forced himself to stand motionless and think. If they had come to kill her, why take away the body? No—she was alive, but kidnapped. Who would kidnap her?

Instantly he thought of the two men who had accosted them at the head of the stairs. One was dead; but had the other come for revenge?

Very damned likely.

Who would know something about the man—Hickson. Maybe Jack English, or the marshal.

Ki rushed out and down the steps. If they had taken her away, they had certainly gone out the back door. He hurried to the back and went out to the alley to look in both directions. Nothing moved—only a cat that stared at him from a nearby fence. He was too late. They might have gone anywhere.

He sighed deeply and went back to the street and down it to the marshal's office. When he turned the knob and entered, a stranger looked up from behind the desk. "Yep?"

"I was looking for Jack English."

"Him and the marshal, they makin' their rounds."

"When will they be back?"

The man shook his head. "Can't tell. You got trouble?"

"Big trouble," Ki said. "Are you a deputy?"

"Nope. Just keep the door open, that's all."

Ki sat down. English and the marshal could be anywhere in the town, in any of the saloons. . . . He would have to wait.

They put Jessica on a horse, and Hickson led the way out of the alley, moving at a walk to attract no attention.

Jessie was wearing jeans. Her hands were tied behind her;

Robby had had to cut her feet loose so she could straddle the animal, but he held the reins and was close beside her.

What did they have in mind?

Probably rape—or worse. Or were they working for someone else? But that was unlikely, wasn't it? Who knew they were here? Over the years they had made enemies, but how could any of them know she and Ki were in Eagle Rock?

Ki would be returning from the saloon, and would come looking for her, but he might be too late. Because after they did whatever they had in mind to do, would they leave her alive? She knew their names and faces. There might not be much law in the town, but murder was always looked down upon.

Hickson led the way out of town and turned off the road into a path leading into the hills.

That probably meant they had a destination.

She was busy pulling and twisting the rope that bound her hands. It seemed to be getting looser. They had tied it in a hurry, and one of the knots was slipping. Every now and then Robby would look at her, but it was very dark and he did not notice what she was doing.

The ground became steeper. Then they were in the trees and it was even darker; she could barely see the horse's ears in front of her. They went another mile or so. The ground leveled off, and suddenly Hickson halted.

She heard him dismount. Then a door squeaked. Robby got down and pulled her off the horse with much handling. She rammed an elbow into his ribs and he grunted and bent forward. She hit him again with the elbow and he spun around. But Hickson was suddenly there, grabbing her and yanking her away.

Her hands came free and she chopped at his wounded arm, hearing him howl. She pushed him, feeling for his pistol, and yanked it from the holster.

Robby was swearing, and as he charged her, she fired twice. He yelled in astonishment and she ran into the dark.

It had all happened in a moment. As she ran she could hear Hickson yelling to Robby: "Don't let her get away!" Robby shouted back in anger that he was shot, dammit!

She tried to follow the trail so she would not run into trees and brush, but it was too dark to see clearly under the trees. She knew they, or one of them, would pursue her on horseback, so she tried to listen for the hoofbeats.

She hoped she had shot Robby in the spot she'd aimed for.

In a few moments she heard the horse. She ducked from the trail and lay motionless in the brush as the horseman galloped past. Then she smiled. He would never find her in the dark; she was the needle in the haystack, and they ought to realize it very soon.

What would they do then?

They would probably go back and station themselves to intercept her when she tried to get back into town.

She got up and went on warily. She wished she had hit Hickson's arm harder. If she had, she might have put him out of action completely. Well, wishing was nice . . .

She had to be wary lest the horseman lay in ambush for her. She was between them now, one in front and one behind, but it was a long time till sunrise. The light would probably put her at a disadvantage; they probably knew the ground and she did not, and there were two of them, with horses.

Her only advantage, aside from the dark, seemed to be that one had a broken arm and the other was wounded, she did not know where. And she had only four more shots in the six-gun.

Moving slowly down the slope, she paused, hearing the horse behind her. It was impossible for a horseman to move noiselessly. He was walking the horse, possibly hoping to flush her out. He probably had no idea what kind of a woman she was.

Jessie waited, standing behind the bole of a husky pine, until the sounds came near. She made out the shadow of the horse, and laid the barrel of the pistol alongside the treetrunk, aiming at the rider.

When she fired, the horse bolted and the rider yelped in surprise. Had she hit him or not? She ducked down, lying flat, and in a moment a fusillade of rifle shots came seeking her. Bullets clipped bark from trees and showered her with twigs. They spanged off branches and did no harm.

She had three bullets left.

When the shots stopped, she got up and moved silently across the trail to the other side.

The moon came out and the two horsemen suddenly charged through the trees where she had been—where her shot had come from. She smiled, hearing them fire at every shadow. She got up and ran down the slope away from them.

Long before the first light, she slipped into the town and went at once to the hotel.

Ki was in his room, fully dressed, pacing the floor. He stared at her when she entered, pistol in hand. "What happened to you?"

She told him the entire story, and he whistled at the end, agreeing with her that they had kidnapped her for revenge. "And Hickson works for Vance Collworth."

"All the more reason I've got to see him," she said.

"I think it's a mistake."

"I've got to know," she said simply.

Chapter 6

It was common knowledge, Kinch told Jessie, that Vance Collworth attended a mine-officials' meeting once a week in Kimberly. Kimberly was about forty miles distant, as the crow flies. He generally stayed overnight and returned the next day.

"How does he go?" Jessie asked.

"Stagecoach," Kinch said. He looked at the clock. "Half-hour from now . . . if he's goin' today." He rubbed his eyes. "I ain't been out. What kinda day is it?"

"Very nice. A good day for traveling."

"What do you want with him, anyways?"

"I just want to talk to him." She went to the door as he shook his head.

The stage station was a dusty building with a large stable and three corrals. Jessica went up the steps into the waiting-room and sat on a bench near a huge black stove with a foot ring. Several men were talking busily in a corner, and a few with parcels and carpetbags were obviously waiting for the stage. They all stared at her.

She ignored them, watching the handlers hitch up a Concord outside the windows. Kinch had told her that the run to

Kimberly was only a one-time-a-week jaunt because of the mail. The government required it, but the stageline did not always go on the same day. However, the run was posted on the door as she entered.

If Vance Collworth was going to the meeting this week, he would go today.

There was a Seth Thomas clock on the wall, and she watched the hands slowly creep around, but Collworth did not appear. The Concord was readied, the horses hitched and baggage tied on . . . then the stagemaster looked into the waiting room.

"Who's goin' to Kimberly?"

The men with the carpet bags jumped up and hurried out to the coach. Jessie rose and went to the door. Maybe this wasn't Collworth's day after all.

The driver climbed up to the box and unwrapped his reins from the brake handle. And as he did so, two men strode into the stage yard. One was a stocky, well-dressed man with steel-rimmed glasses. He nodded to the stagemaster and climbed into the coach, followed by the second man. The door slammed and the stage moved out to the street and turned left.

Jessie stared after it. When the stagemaster came to the door she asked, "Who was that man?"

"Why, that was Vance Collworth, ma'am." He tipped his hat and went by her.

Jessie went down the steps to the yard and out to the street. The man she had seen was not Vance Collworth! He was an impostor!

In the hotel she told Ki what she had seen. He was surprised. "But it explains a lot of things," he mused. "That's why Nails knew he wouldn't see you. Nails knew he wouldn't know you."

"There was a resemblance to the real Collworth—but it definitely was another man. What does it mean, Ki?"

"It means something has happened to the real one. Either he's dead or he's being held somewhere."

"It also means the real one had something to lose—something they wanted."

"This town?"

"Maybe."

Ki said, "Remember Jack English told us that Collworth seldom appeared in public. That was so no one could expose him. And you say he looked something like the real Collworth—maybe enough to fool a casual acquaintance."

"And maybe he had the doubters run out of town."

Ki nodded. "Probably. Or killed."

Jessie sighed. "What do we do now? If we tell everyone what we know, they'll kill *us*. He's surrounded himself with a tough gang."

"Let's try not to get killed. Where's the nearest United States marshal? We could send a letter—"

"Do you think they watch the mails?"

"Hm. Probably. Maybe we can send a letter out with someone."

Jessica shrugged. "If we can find someone."

"Do you trust Jack English?"

She hesitated. "I'd like to. But I'm sure Collworth pays his salary. I'd have to talk to him again." She rubbed her cheek absently. "But Nails said we were to be out of town by today. Can he make that stick?"

"If he can find us, maybe." He gave her a long look. "This changes everything, you know. Do we want to get into this fight?"

"I owe it to my father to find out what's happened to Vance—the real Vance. I'd never feel right if I walked away from this."

Ki smiled. "Then that's what we'll do. We'll find out what's happened."

She smiled.

"But we can't stay here in the hotel," Ki said. "Nails will send his gang here to run us out of town. The best thing is for us not to be here when they arrive."

"I'll pack our things."

He nodded. "I'll tell Kinch we're moving on—I'll say we're going to return to Texas. You come down to the stable and I'll have the horses saddled."

"Good."

Kinch was surprised to see them go. "Texas, huh? I got a

cousin'r two in Fort Worth. Ain't seen 'em in ten year. Ought to get back there one day..."

In the stable Ki saddled both horses, and when Jessie came down he tied on their blanket rolls and canteens. Jessie looked at the sky. "I hope the weather holds."

"It will." He leaned on the horse. "We could cut across lots and get into the hills from here—but why not let them see us go? They'll think we're scared out, and maybe they'll forget about us for a while."

She agreed. "Let's do that. If we suddenly disappear they may come looking for us."

They walked the horses out to the street and turned right, moving past the Golden Slipper. With his hat pulled low, Ki saw two men come to a window and watch them for a moment. Good. They had been seen. He said as much to Jessica softly, and she nodded.

It was a fine day, as she had said—a good day for traveling. They left the town behind, still walking the horses. Ki wondered if Nails would send a man to see where they went, but apparently he did not. Ki smiled at the sky. He and Jessie had been underestimated before.

They had gone probably five miles when they came round a bend and saw the four men. Three were attacking a fourth. One of the three, Ki thought, he had seen in the Slipper, a young, rangy man with a whiskery face.

The three were afoot, beating an older man, kicking him mercilessly. Jessie drew her pistol and Ki spurred forward at once. The attackers swung around, hearing the horses, and one pulled a pistol and was about to fire. Ki's *shuriken* ripped into his throat and he fell with a strangling cry.

Jessie fired, barely over the heads of the others, and they stood motionless, staring at their dead companion and the pool of blood about his head. They had not heard the shot that killed him.

"Put him on his horse and get out of here," Jessie said.

Her voice seemed to jolt them, and they both frowned and looked hard at her. One man nudged his horse closer. "Hey—she's only a woman!"

Half-turned away from her, he went for his gun and Jessie shot him in the leg. He dropped the reins, stumbled, and fell to his knees. The revolver skittered across the rutted road, and the horse pranced away.

The old man they had been beating rolled onto his back with a groan.

Jessica said again, "On your horses." She cocked the pistol with easy confidence.

The whiskery man nodded, hard eyes on them. Grunting, he lifted the body and slung it over a horse, then helped the hurt man to mount, both of them growling and swearing under their breath.

Ki got down and picked up the pistol, shoving it into his belt. The whiskery man eyed him, mounted his own horse and, without another word, rode toward the town slowly.

Standing in the center of the road, Ki watched them go, ready for tricks, but there were none.

Jessie got down and went to the old man. Gently lifting his head, she gave him water from her canteen. He was wearing a worn checked shirt and jeans; his boots were battered but serviceable. He looked like an aging rancher. He thanked her for the water and sat up, wincing, sucking in his breath.

"I am Fernando Diaz," he told her. He would have many bruises to show, but the beating had broken no bones. "They followed me from the town . . ."

"Do you know them?"

The old man shook his head. "I have never seen them before."

"Then why would they beat you?"

"A man wants our land—maybe they work for him."

Ki knelt by them. "Who is this man?"

"His name is Jonas Clark."

"But isn't he a cattleman?"

Diaz nodded. "He is head of the cattlemen's organization, which has offered us money for our land. But we refused."

Ki looked at Jessie. How many times had they heard this same kind of story? She shook her head sadly. The old man was in his seventies, a sheepherder, he told them. He gestured toward the hills, saying he lived there with his family.

"Only some of our land is good for cattle," Diaz said. "But it is closer to the town. Maybe they want it for that reason."

"Have you ever met this man Clark?"

"No." Diaz tried to get up. He nearly fell, but Ki supported him; Jessie brought his horse and he clung to the saddle, his face pale. He was obviously worse off than he thought.

"How far is your home?" Ki asked.

Diaz closed his eyes and took a long breath. "Eight miles." He tried to smile at her. "I will be all right."

"I don't think so," Jessie said. "You are hurt."

"Let me rest a moment."

Jessie looked at Ki. "We cannot let him go alone. We must help him home."

"No, no, no," the old man protested. "I will be all right. If you will help me on the horse . . ."

"We will make sure you are all right," Jessie said firmly. They helped him to mount.

"Now, tell us the way," Ki said.

★

Chapter 7

They left the road at the old man's direction and found a worn trail that wound into the hills, following their contours. Twice they crossed a hurrying stream, then climbed a steep zigzag and came out onto a beautiful meadow which was dotted with white sheep.

Immediately they were surrounded by several young men with rifles. One, a brooding young man with dark eyes, regarded them suspiciously. Diaz spoke to them rapidly in a strange language, and they all smiled.

They were taken immediately to a group of houses that sat among lofty pines, overlooking the meadow, and Diaz was helped down and carried tenderly into one of the houses.

One of the young men explained. "We are Basques. Our grandparents came to this country looking for peace. We have always been herders, and we cause no trouble to anyone. Tell me about the men who beat my father."

Jessica explained how they had come upon the men, and how they had driven the three off, killing one. "I am afraid his death will cause you trouble . . ."

The young man smiled sadly. "We have had little but trouble since we settled here a few years ago. Someone wants our land. We think it is Jonas Clark, the cattleman, but we cannot be positive."

"Why would he want it?" Ki asked. "It is excellent for sheep but not so good for cattle. Are there other meadows like this around here?"

"Yes, three or four, scattered in the mountains. We move the sheep from one to the other."

The young man's name was Carlos. His older brother was named Ramon, he told them. Ramon was the hot-tempered one, and they always feared he would ride into Jonas Clark's range one day and start shooting.

When they went to the house they found that Ramon had gone to bring back a woman who was skilled in medicine and healing. The elder Diaz was in bed, his wife sitting beside him. She came to embrace Jessie and thank Ki for the rescue.

"Our house is yours."

A young woman spoke from the doorway. "There is food on the table. Come, you must eat with us."

They turned. Ki was astonished at her beauty. Mrs. Diaz said, "This is my daughter, Carmelita."

Carmelita smiled. "Thank you for what you did for my father. They would have killed him."

Ki sat down, basking in her smile. Had he ever seen anyone so lovely? She had dark hair like her mother, and huge, expressive eyes. She was dressed, also like her mother, in a simple gown, gathered at the waist. He knew Jessie was looking at him, but he could not take his eyes off her.

The fare was simple: mutton and beans, with fresh-baked bread. Carmelita explained that they baked bread every week, and Ki hung on her words, forgetting to eat. Jessica had to nudge him under the table.

Jessie asked, "Have you protested to the sheriff that you're being threatened?"

"Oh yes, certainly," Carlos said. "Many times."

"We think they ignore us," Carmelita offered. Her dark eyes flashed. "We are only Basques, after all."

"Who is the sheriff?" Ki asked.

"His name is John Collins. But his office is in Kimberly, a

long way from here. One of his deputies comes to Eagle Rock now and then but he never stays long."

Ki said, "What about the town marshal, Ned Hilton . . . is he an honest man?"

Carlos shrugged. "We are not sure. He has no jurisdiction here in the mountains, but Collworth helps pay his salary. He is hired by the Merchants' Association."

"That makes him suspect," Carmelita said. She rose and went in to look at her father again.

Jessica and Ki went out to the veranda; Carlos followed them. "What will you do now? Can you return to the town?"

Ki shook his head. "They ordered us out."

"Nails?"

"Yes." Ki smiled thinly. "We spread the word that we were returning to Texas. Let's hope they believe it."

Carlos lit a cheroot and puffed. "You do not intend to go to Texas?"

"No," Jessie said. "We are staying—at least for a time."

Carlos extended his arm. "You heard my mother. Our house is yours. As a matter of fact we have several houses." He pointed. "That one is empty at the moment. It is yours if you want it."

It was a smaller log house, well chinked, with a fieldstone chimney. When they went inside Jessie saw that it had been cared for. It was swept out and smelled clean. The furniture was heavy and obviously homemade, but it was very serviceable. She glanced at Ki who nodded. They would move in—for the moment.

The two surviving toughs rode into town, leading the horse that carried the carcass of the third. They stopped at the office of Doc Hamblin. Harris, the whiskered one, half-carried his wounded companion inside and laid him on the table Hamblin indicated.

"Gunshot," Harris said as the doc began to untie the crude bandage. "Patch him up and send the bill to Vance."

Hamblin nodded absently, moving a light to see the wound better.

Harris went back outside and rode to the undertaker's door. He yelled for assistance, and a man came out and helped him carry in the body of the man Ki's *shuriken* had felled.

"Put him in a pine box."

The undertaker searched the pockets of the dead man and found twenty dollars and a few coins. He smiled. "This'll buy him a coat of stain on the box. Look real perty." He put the money in a drawer. "The marshal know about this shootin'?"

Harris went to the door, scratching his whiskers. "His name was Nathan Smith—anyway that's what he called himself."

"How old was he? You got to put dates on the headstone. Folks expects it."

"He was about thirty-five. You can subtract, can't you?"

The undertaker nodded.

Harris said, "I'll tell the marshal about the shootin' when I see him."

"All right. I'll give him a wood headpiece. It'll look fine." The undertaker fingered the dead man's empty holster. "Where's his gun?"

"I'll take it back to Nails. What else you need?"

"Guess that's all." He regarded the body morosely. "He was thirty-five? He looks older."

Harris shrugged. "Make 'im forty then." He waved and went out to his horse. He rode to the Slipper and asked to see Nails. A bartender pointed him to the downstairs office.

Nails was sitting behind the desk when Harris went in, and he was annoyed that one of his men had died. "How the hell did that happen?"

"They got the drop on us."

"You tellin' me a chink and a girl killed Nate, shot Link in the goddamn leg and drove you-all off?"

Harris shuffled his feet. "The chink threw some kinda knife at Nate. Took 'im in the throat. Jesus! I never saw nothing so fast!"

Nails's voice was sarcastic. "Faster'n a bullet?"

"Well . . ."

"Git outta here. Go get Ned Hilton—tell 'im I want to see him." Nails motioned to the door.

He watched Harris hurry out. He slumped at the desk, staring at the opposite wall without seeing it. He didn't give a damn about Nate Smith, but it was bad to have one of his men killed. It was like it was undermining his authority. Also the county sheriff usually heard about shooting deaths—it was hard to keep them quiet. And one day he might come to investigate.

That would be bad for business.

Ned Hilton was in his office, half asleep, feet up on an opened drawer of the desk. He yawned, hearing Nails wanted to see him. "What about?"

"He didn't say."

Hilton took his hat and went out, grumbling to himself. Nails never had anything good to say. . . .

And this time was no exception. Nails said, "I want you to pull in Fernando Diaz on a charge of murder. Take some men and go up in the—"

"What! Old Diaz, the sheepherder?"

"He's the one. You get a posse together and bring him in—unless he gives you trouble."

Hilton frowned. "Who'd he murder?"

"Nate Smith."

"When'd this happen?"

"Couple hours ago, out on the road. His body's over at the undertaker's right now."

"Jesus! Did anybody see it?"

"Harris did. So did Link. He got shot in the leg."

Hilton took a long breath. "For Crissakes, Nails, old Diaz never carries a gun. I never seen him with one. How'd he shoot them both?"

Nails growled. "I didn't ask you to stand there and question me! I told you t'get out and bring in Diaz. You got trouble with your ears, Marshal?"

Hilton sighed. "All right." He walked to the door, glanced back, and went out.

Chapter 8

Sheep had been killed in an upper meadow. The culprits were unknown, but it had been done under cover of night. They had suffered three such attacks, Carmelita told Ki, and offered to show him where the latest had taken place.

They took a winding path that led up a gorge that branched after several miles and led them to a lovely tree-girt meadow, as peaceful a scene as Ki had ever gazed upon.

All the sheep had been moved to the lower meadow, she told him, because it was easier to guard them. Her brothers and several other men constantly rode the perimeter with rifles, day and night, ready for trouble.

"My father has a friend, an Indian, who tracked the sheep-killers back to the town. So we know they came from Eagle Rock."

"But the cattleman, Jonas Clark, is not in Eagle Rock."

"But the men he sent could have started from there and returned there . . . to make us think the killers were sent by Collworth."

Ki smiled. "It gets complicated, doesn't it?" He leaned on the horn of his saddle, looking at the valley and the surrounding mountains. "It is important to know one's enemies. Who has most to gain by driving you off this land?"

She hesitated. "We think it is Jonas Clark."

"But you are not positive?"

She sighed. "No, not absolutely positive."

"Then this Mr. Clark should be asked."

"Yes, but who will go?" She pursed her lips. "My father is in no condition . . . and we cannot send Ramon! Perhaps Carlos can do it. But—" She bit her lip.

"What is it?"

"I know my father will not want him to go. If Jonas Clark will send men to kill our sheep, will he not kill my brother?"

Ki dismounted, and took her hand when she jumped down. They walked across the grass in silence for several moments. Then he said, "Maybe you should go."

She looked at him in surprise. "Me?"

"I will go with you."

She halted and turned to him. "You would do this for us?"

"Of course."

Impulsively she moved close and kissed him. "You are a good man. I think I like you very much."

"I like you too." He kissed her and held her for a moment. Then she stepped back. Taking his hand, she said, "Over there, by those rocks, we found the dead sheep."

Ramon returned with the old woman, who carried a bag of herbs and vials containing various healing substances. She was very dark, with braided black hair and the serene face of one who has few doubts.

When they took her to Fernando's bed, she shooed them all away, asking only for a basin of hot water and some cloths with which to wash the wounds.

Ramon went out to the veranda and paced back and forth, smoking a black cheroot, his spurs jingling on the hard boards. Jessica sat quietly in a chair at the far end of the wide veranda and when he noticed her, Ramon stopped his pacing.

"Where is your friend?"

"Your sister is showing him the upper meadow where the sheep were killed."

Ramon stared at her. "They went alone?"

"Yes . . . why?"

"It is—it is dangerous!"

Jessie shrugged. "She did not seem to think so."

"Carmelita is sometimes a foolish girl." Ramon walked down the steps and stared at the mountain. Then he seemed to make up his mind. He tossed the cheroot away and hurried to his horse. Mounting, he galloped up the trail to the meadow.

He was incensed. The idea of a Chinese taking his sister away alone! What could they be doing! He had heard that Chinamen went crazy when with a woman. If this one was taking advantage of his sister—no matter how much he had helped their father—he would kill him!

Ramon galloped the horse the entire way and ran into the meadow to pull up in its center, his horse heaving and panting with the exertion. Ramon was astonished. His sister and the man were walking across the grass, a dozen feet apart, fully clothed. They both halted and stared at him.

Then Carmelita ran toward him. "Is something the matter—has something happened to father?"

Ramon shook his head, confused. "No . . . no . . ."

"Then what is it?"

Ki said in an even tone, "He was worried about you."

She looked at him. "What?"

Ramon found his voice. "Yes . . . I was worried. You are a—a long way from the house—" He cleared his throat. "Someone might have—"

"Ramon! You know I come here often alone! What is the matter with you?"

"It is because you are with me," Ki said. "I will get the horses and we will go back at once." He turned away.

Carmelita stared after him, then turned an angry face to her brother. "What were you thinking, Ramon? That I am a *puta?*"

"No, no, of course not!"

"This is the man who saved our father! You are acting like a fool!"

Ramon's lips tightened. He yanked the horse's head around and dug in his spurs. She stood, hands on hips, and watched him gallop from the meadow. Yes, he was a fool.

When Ki brought the horses she said, "I apologize for my brother. He is a hot-head. . . ."

"You are not responsible for your brother. Do not let it worry you." He handed her the reins. "He is no different from many others."

She regarded him for a moment, then smiled. "You are a very unusual man, Ki."

He made her a little bow. "And you are a very beautiful woman."

She said, "You may kiss me again."

Jack English was assigned by the marshal to bring in Fernando Diaz. "You know where he lives."

"He has two sons who will never let me bring him out of the mountains without a fight."

"Then take some men. Get yourself a posse. Vance wants him charged with murder."

"Vance does?"

"Well . . . Nails does. Nails says Diaz shot and killed Nate Smith and shot Link in the leg."

English laughed. "Old Diaz never carries a gun! It must have been someone else."

"Maybe it was, but Nails wants Diaz charged. Then a jury will decide."

"A rigged jury? Diaz will never have a chance."

Hilton shouted, "Do like you're told, goddammit!"

Jack English sighed deeply and went out to his horse. Ned was upset, and it was obvious that he knew Diaz wasn't guilty—or it wouldn't bother him.

He headed for the mountain path, worrying it. Diaz could not have shot Nate Smith; it just wasn't possible. And if he took a posse into the mountains he would start a war with the Basques. Ned Hilton should know that.

Ned must be farther under Nails's thumb than he'd thought.

When he reached the foothills he walked the horse, following the well used trail. In two hours he came to an outcropping where the trail became a narrow path, winding between the rocks.

As he entered it he heard a voice: "Stop there!"

Jack reined in at once, hands at shoulder height.

The voice asked, "What d'you want?"

"I came to see Fernando Diaz."

"You're the deputy marshal in Eagle Rock . . ."

English nodded. "I come as a friend."

There was a long silence and Jack waited patiently. Then the voice said, "Come ahead . . . slow."

Chapter 9

Jessica Starbuck was astonished to see Jack English. He came riding to the house with Ramon and two men armed with shotguns.

"Hello!" English said in surprise. "I didn't know you were here." He got down and walked up the steps. "I heard Nails told you and Ki to get out of town."

She smiled. "We were frightened to death so we hurried."

He laughed. "I imagine you were." He glanced to Ramon and back to her. "So it was you—and Ki—who shot Nate Smith."

"A very shrewd guess, Mr. English."

"And then you brought Mr. Diaz home."

She nodded. "Right again."

Ramon asked, "Where is Carlos?"

"Here," Carlos said, stepping onto the porch from the house. "Hello, Jack."

English smiled. "Good morning. May I see your father? He is well, I hope."

"He is much better, thanks." Carlos nodded and indicated the door.

Fernando Diaz was sitting up in bed, several pillows behind him. He wore a blue woolen shirt and they could see the white of a bandage at the neck. He was alone when they went in and his eyes widened, seeing Jack English.

"You have come to arrest me?"

Jack laughed. "Not I, sir. But others would like to."

"Why have you come?" Carlos asked.

"To tell you what I can. My orders are to bring you into town." English shrugged. "Of course that is impossible. They want to put you on trial for the death of Nate Smith—but I know you did not kill him."

Diaz looked at Jessica. "That is true."

Jack said, "I will go back and tell them I could not find you. But you must not stay here."

"Why not?"

"Because I fear that Marshal Hilton will bring a posse. Nails employs a number of hard cases. There would be a battle—" He shrugged. "People would be killed. It would be better if you went into hiding for the time being. Is there somewhere you can go?"

"Several places," Carlos said.

Jack put up a hand. "Do not tell me."

Carlos smiled. "I wasn't going to."

"I cannot anticipate Nails. I don't know what he'll do next, so you must stay out of his reach."

Diaz nodded solemnly. "Thank you, my friend. We will take precautions."

Jessica spoke up. "I imagine there's a good deal more behind this, isn't there?"

The older man nodded again. "I believe Collworth wants our land. Why else would they try to frame me?"

"He will not get the land," Carlos said grimly. "We will fight him every step of the way. And we know every inch of the mountains. They do not."

Jack English spent the rest of the day as their guest. He told them it would bolster his story of hunting for their father.

That evening he went down the mountain with Carlos as guide.

• • •

A suitable place for their father was discussed after Jack had left. There were several hunting cabins in the mountains, most well hidden. When they decided upon one, it was agreed to keep the fact secret among themselves. One could not be too careful.

In the morning after breakfast two mules were packed with necessities, and Diaz and his wife, Dolores, rode with Carlos to the cabin. No one would ever find them, Carmelita told Jessie, unless they wanted to be found.

There were other Basque families living in the little settlement, the houses scattered among the trees in no particular order. There was no street. Ramon and a group of his neighbors were patrolling the foothills, and had been for months. If Nails sent a posse after the older Diaz, Ramon would not be taken by surprise. It would be the other way round.

Carlos would stay a day with his parents, he told them, to get them settled.

When he had gone, Jessica talked with Carmelita. "Someone should go to the sheriff. It *is* a crime to kill sheep, to say nothing of the attack on your father."

"You are right. I must go myself."

"The sheriff is at Kimberly. That is several days' journey from here."

Carmelita smiled. "I have been there before. Ki said that we should find out if Jonas Clark is behind these attacks."

"How would you do that?"

"Ask him."

Jessie laughed. "Ki is very direct. What else did he say?"

"He offered to go with me."

When Ki came into the house they told him what they were discussing . . . and Ki shook his head. "I have changed my mind about going with you. I think I must go alone."

She was disappointed. "Why?"

"It might prove too dangerous for two people."

"I can ride and shoot!" Carmelita protested.

"If we have to dodge bullets or hide, it is easier for one to find a hole than two. Also it would pain me to see bullet holes in that lovely skin."

"You are just saying that. I cannot imagine you crawling into a hole."

Ki smiled and shrugged. "There is a time for shooting and a time for hiding. It depends on the situation and the people. Oh, yes . . . I will need a letter from you to show that I go to the sheriff on your behalf."

Carmelita sighed. "Very well. I will see that you get it."

Ki walked out to the veranda with Jessie. She said, "I do not like you to be away too long."

"I should be back in four days."

"I have a feeling these people will be attacked in force before long."

Ki looked at the sky. "While I am in Kimberly I will write to the United States marshal. He may not know what kind of a town Eagle Rock is."

"And the sheriff should know . . . if he does not already."

"He and his deputies may be spread very thin." Ki rubbed his jaw. "We have seen this before where the people in power skimp on law enforcement." He smiled at her. "Speaking of law, I'm glad Jack English came up to see us. Despite the people he works for, I think he is an honest man."

"When you go, don't go through the town."

Ki smiled. "I will go around it."

"And wait for nightfall. Yes, I think Jack is an honest man too."

Ned Hilton hated the job he was doing—and could not seem to get out of it. He had drifted into Eagle Rock needing a job. Being a peace officer was easy work most times, but Eagle Rock was a bad town. He hadn't realized it at first. Maybe he should have, considering how easily he had been hired.

The town marshal he was replacing had been dry-gulched a few days before he'd arrived. They told him the man had had many enemies.

He'd applied to the Merchants' Association, had shown them credentials proving he'd been a lawman in several towns and had been a deputy sheriff as well. He'd been hired at once, at the first meeting. The president of the association even took him downstairs and bought him a drink.

They seemed awfully eager to hire him.

Jack English had ridden into town about a week later. He

had also been a peace officer, he told Ned. Ned had hired him as deputy.

It hadn't worried Ned that it was a tough town; he'd been in towns like this before, and he was good with a gun. It was when he met Nails, Vance Collworth's right-hand man, that he began to want out.

He knew, almost at first glance, that Nails was vicious, and would do anything to further his own ends. Nails had taken him into his private office and explained what Ned was to do. He was to swear before the local justice of the peace, so it would be recorded, that he had seen a certain hombre rob another man.

"I saw nothing of the sort!"

"Did I ask you that? You do as you're told."

"But—"

Nails's silky voice said, "I wouldn't argue if I was you. Do like I tell you." He pointed to the door.

But it was not until a case of obvious murder had come along, and Nails had ordered him to be a witness for the killer—thus freeing the man—that Ned had discovered the worst. The very worst.

In the month or so that he'd been marshal, Nails had learned about Ned's two daughters at school in Missouri. Nails overlooked nothing. Ned would testify the way he was asked, or the girls would suffer.

Beaten, Ned had done as ordered. Then he'd stayed drunk for three days.

When he finally sobered up he spent hours planning how he could have the girls sent somewhere else—his wife was dead—but he had too little money to pay someone. How could he accomplish it at a distance anyhow?

Then Nails had let him know that the girls were watched constantly.

Nails said, "Don't be a jackass, Hilton. Do the job as you're told and you'll get along fine." He pointed a finger. "But cross me and you're dead."

Ned believed every word.

Ned knew that Nails would be very annoyed when Jack came back from the hills without the older Diaz. Fernando was nowhere around. Jack said, "I think they sent him away.

Those Basques are very damned close-mouthed, you know. They wouldn't tell me a thing."

"You should have taken a dozen men."

"It wouldn't have helped. We'd have had a battle royal and I wouldn't have learned the little I did."

"Maybe . . ."

"I think Diaz is hundreds of miles away by now."

Ned sighed deeply. Probably so. Certainly the Basques weren't stupid. But would Nails accept it?

Nails didn't like it at all, didn't believe any of it. He cursed Ned and finally sent him away. Ned was happy to get out. Nails made him very nervous.

That night he went to bed drunk again.

★

Chapter 10

Carlos returned from the mountain hideaway saying his parents were comfortable and safe. He would return every few days with supplies and whatever they wished. His father's wounds were healing nicely. He was tough as shoe leather and would be good as new in no time.

Ki slept for several hours, waking when Carmelita sat on the edge of the cot with the promised letter, which Carlos had written out in a fine copperplate.

"You must take no chances," she said. "You are going there for us. I couldn't bear it if you—"

He pulled her to him, embracing her warmly. "No one knows I am going, so no one will be looking for me. *Verdad?*" He kissed her. "I will be back before you know it."

She whispered, nuzzling him, "*I* will know it."

He felt her take a long breath, nestling even closer to him. His hand slid down her curving back as her lips sought his again. In another moment he would be lost—he knew she could feel him stiffening. . . .

He managed to say, "This is not the place . . ."

He was surprised when she reluctantly agreed, with another long breath. "Come back to me . . . come back to me . . ."

"I will," he promised, meaning every word. He glanced at the window; it was dark out. He embraced her again, tasting her kisses. Then he lifted her aside and got out of the bed to dress.

She walked to the stable with him. He was saddling the horse when Jessica appeared.

"I went to wake you, but you were already up." She smiled at Carmelita.

Ki said, "I am a light sleeper."

"See that you watch your backtrail."

He swung up and smiled at them: two beautiful women to see him off. Carmelita was a pale shadow in the night. He touched her hand and walked the bay horse from the stable.

At the rocks he met Ramon and Carlos. Carlos was examining his cinch. Then he mounted as Ramon said, "It is better that you do not go alone."

"I will be—"

"I am going with you," Carlos said. "Let us not argue about it. Besides, my presence will provide proof."

"I have your letter." Ki patted his inside pocket.

"Someone could say that it was forged." Carlos smiled. "But he could not say it to me because I wrote it."

"We are agreed," Ramon said, "that he will go. That is the end of it."

Ki looked at them and shrugged. "Very well. Then let us be on our way. But while we go you must think of a reason to tell your sister why *she* could not go."

"Hmm." Carlos frowned, then brightened. "I have several days to think of an answer."

Ki would have taken the trail down the mountain to the town, then skirted it carefully. But Carlos knew another way. He had been born in the mountains, and they had no secrets from him. He was well acquainted with every ravine and cave and nook for fifty miles around. He led Ki through a tunnel of high brush, down a sandy dry stream, and along a game trail, leaving the town far behind.

On the flatlands at last, they loped the horses, making excellent time. Kimberly, Carlos said, was in the low hills to the west. It was now a stage division point, a crossroads town, and in decades past had been an Indian trading post. Now it was also the county seat.

They continued through the night, stopping several times for short rests, walking the horses the way the cavalry did. They reached the town the next day before noon and went directly to the sheriff's office.

The town was a sprawling place, scattered like wild seed over a shallow valley, watered by a cold stream, encircled by low hills.

The sheriff, John Collins, was not in. A clerk told them he had been called somewhere, he was not exactly sure where, but he would be back by morning. "If he ain't, then you kin talk to his chief deputy. He'll be here then too."

"We'll be in tomorrow," Ki said.

They had a meal in one of the two restaurants—tough beef and boiled potatoes, with coffee. Afterward they went to sit in tilted-back chairs in front of the Kimberly Hotel where they rented rooms. Watching the street, Ki asked, "How well do you know Jack English?"

"Only casually."

"He seems like a good, solid, honest man. Why does he work as deputy marshal in a town like Eagle Rock? He must know his bosses are no good."

Carlos made a face. "I really never thought about it."

"He could surely get a job anywhere else, don't you think?"

"Yes, I guess he could."

"Have you had trouble with Ned Hilton before?"

"No. He has no jurisdiction in the mountains. I don't believe he's ever been up where we live. He'd have no reason."

"I meant when you go to town for supplies."

Carlos shook his head. "No. Only the one time, when you rescued my father. One of us goes to the post office once a week. Father had gone that day."

Ki thought about it, scratching his neck. Could that have been an opening move in some plan?

"Has there been anything different—in the last few months?"

Carlos considered. "Well, you know about the sheep that were killed. . . ."

"Yes."

"There was one odd thing—I had almost forgotten it. We also found some evidences of prospecting."

Ki looked at his companion. "Tell me."

"Well, no one has ever found minerals on our side of the mountain, that we know of. All the silver mines are to the west of us. But someone has dug a few holes here and there —and then covered them up."

"Covered them up?"

"Yes. We figured he'd found nothing and didn't want us to spot the holes so we'd know someone had been there."

Ki smiled. "So someone came into the mountains and you didn't know it?"

Carlos pulled at his chin. "It's a huge area and there're only a few of us. We can't be everywhere."

"And he probably came at night."

"Yes, and whoever he was, he didn't follow any trails and he probably camped without fires. It wouldn't have been that difficult."

Ki nodded. "Anything else you can think of?"

Carlos pursed his lips. "Well, Ramon had a run-in with Nails a time ago. . . ."

"How long ago?"

"Umm, maybe four–five months. They had some words in the street, but people came between them and it came to nothing."

"Is Nails good with a gun?"

"We're told he is. But so is Ramon. My brother, bless him, is afraid of nothing. It worries us."

"So your sister told me."

They sat gazing at the street for a while, then finally went up to bed. Ki had a tiny room at the back, with a single grimy window with heavy curtains made out of flowered oilcloth. Through it he had a fine view of a row of stables.

The bed was hard but not lumpy. He undressed and lay for a time staring at the dark ceiling. The fact that Vance Collworth was *not* really Vance Collworth, but someone impersonating him, was bothersome. There had to be a very good reason behind all that—probably money. Could it be connected with the Basques and their land?

If not, why had the older Diaz been accosted and beaten? Had they intended to kill him? Was it a first move against the land?

Of course it could be a move against *them,* and not the land. Aliens were not always well accepted—as he knew himself, being half Japanese. There were two things against his new friends: they were Basques and they were sheepherders.

In the morning they had breakfast in the same restaurant and then went on to the sheriff's office and found Collins in. He was a beefy, bland-faced man in his fifties who greeted them pleasantly, and who frowned slightly when he heard they had come from Eagle Rock.

"Not my favorite town in the county," he said, pointing to chairs. He fussed in a drawer for a cigar and struck a match. "What can I do for you?"

Ki gave him a brief history of the Basques and their situation, and the sheriff nodded, puffing smoke. He looked closely at Carlos as Ki mentioned the sheep that had been killed.

"How much of the mountain do you own, son?"

Carlos held up his hand. "There are five of us with a hundred and sixty acres each. It is the area closest to the town. I have the homestead papers with me if you wish to see them."

Sheriff Collins waved the cigar. "I got no reason to doubt you. But I got to tell you one thing. You have no evidence. You don't know who is doin' these things to you. You can make only a vague complaint."

Ki said, "And you do not have the men to investigate."

Collins frowned at him, then nodded. "That is the situation, yes. The damn county's got a poor budget. I'm always strapped for men." He shook his head. "If you had something a man could get his teeth into—then I could justify a man'r two lookin' into things."

"You mean we must do your work for you?" Carlos asked.

Collins's eyes slitted. "Don't get riled up, son. We do what we can."

"Do you know about Nails?"

"His name is Harry Pike. Yes, I know about him." He puffed hard on the cigar. "This ain't the time to talk about Harry Pike."

Carlos let out his breath. "Well, poor or not, I want to make a complaint, Sheriff. I want it on the record. I am sure there will be more trouble."

"Very well." Collins pulled out a drawer and selected a form. He opened a case, took out glasses and put them on, found a pencil and looked at Carlos. "First spell your name. . . ."

When he had finished he rose and shook hands with them and they walked back to the hotel. "A long trip for nothing," Carlos said.

"I think he told you the truth. He doesn't have enough deputies."

The hotel clerk on duty was an older man, with iron-gray hair and thick glasses that kept sliding down his nose. In answer to Ki's question he said the United States marshal had his office in Belmer, a town on the railroad about sixty miles north of Kimberly.

"I seen a pitcher of him in the weekly," he told them. "Maybe a year ago. Fine-lookin' man." That was all he knew. The marshal had never been in Kimberly. "Least not while I been clerkin' here."

Carlos asked, "What do folks think of Sheriff Collins?"

"Good man. Honest as hell. Never promises nothing he can't deliver come election time. He been sheriff three–four times as I recollect."

"Does he get out in the county?"

"You bet. Prob'ly two weeks out'n the month he makes rounds. Don't sell him short. We think a good deal of him around here." The clerk grinned. 'Course he gettin' a little ass-heavy in the last couple years . . . but that don't affect his headbones."

They thanked the clerk for his opinions, and then Ki sat by a window and composed a letter to the U.S. marshal, acquainting him with the facts. He bought a stamp and posted it, wondering how many such letters the man received in a month's time.

When he went to bed that night he lay awake for a time, thinking about Carmelita. It made a difference, being able to think of someone like that.

★

Chapter 11

Jack English was not his real name. He had boarded a train in Knoxville in one hell of a hurry, two jumps ahead of the city police. He didn't know where the train was bound, just so it left Tennessee. And he selected a name from a newspaper, just to have it handy.

An upright citizen had been gunned down in a neighborhood bar, and Jack had had the unfortunate luck to resemble the gunman as described by half a dozen barflies. His luck had almost run out when he had happened to be in the vicinity of the bar at the time and the police had nabbed him.

There were two of them, elderly men, and Jack had quickly knocked them both down and sprinted away before they could get their whistles out.

He had no money for a lawyer and no inclination to spend months behind bars waiting for a trial date for a crime he had not committed. He knew about jails firsthand, and they were not his favorite places.

His real name was Jack Bannister. He had been a soldier; a bartender, between good jobs; and a deputy sheriff. Once he had worked for a daily newspaper in the pressroom and once he had been a saloon bouncer.

He read the newspapers as the train puffed its way west. The killer was still at large, the papers said. His arrest was expected momentarily, however.

Jack got off the train and took a stage into the sticks. When the last newspaper he bought no longer carried the story, he got off the stage and he was in Eagle Rock. He decided he had come far enough. Tennessee was a long way behind him; in a few years they would forget, he hoped. He would spend those years in an out-of-the-way place. And Eagle Rock was about as out-of-the-way as one could get.

By city standards it was a wide spot in the road. He put his new-bought valise under the bed of one of the five boarding-houses in town and settled in.

And after a day or two he realized what Eagle Rock really was, a town under the thumb of Vance Collworth. He wondered how long he could stand it.

But he needed a job, and when he walked into the Town Marshal's office, Ned Hilton gave him a smile. And after a talk, hired him.

Ned was a good sort in his way. Of course, he drank too much. . . .

Then, about three months after he had arrived in Eagle Rock, Jack met a man named Homer Gregg. Gregg came to the marshal's office one early evening to say he was having trouble with a neighbor, and he asked Jack to come with him to straighten it out.

Jack picked up a Winchester and followed Gregg to a house on the edge of town. Gregg unlocked the door and they went inside. Jack was surprised to find the house only half furnished. No one lived there.

"What is this?"

Gregg smiled. "It's a place to talk, away from everybody else." He gestured. "Pull up a chair."

"Talk about what?"

Gregg sat in a ladder-backed chair. "Sit down and let me tell you a story."

Jack shrugged. He sat and pulled out the makin's. "You going to talk in the dark?"

"Yes. First let me tell you that we've watched you since you came to town and—"

"Who's 'we'?"

"Several of us." Gregg waved a hand. "We think you're straight. I mean, not one of Collworth's gang." He smiled thinly. "If you are, you're damned slick about it."

"I'm not." Jack finished the cigarette but did not light it. "What're you getting at?"

"What we're getting at is law and order. We want *real* law for this town and the area. Vance Collworth and Nails run things their way—with Nails's gunmen backing him up. We are going to change that."

"It may not be easy."

"We know."

"Who do you represent?"

"A number of men who are interested in the area's future and not the short-term dollar. We have seen operations like Collworth's before. When he pulls every dollar he can out of Eagle Rock he'll move on and do the same thing somewhere else."

"You could wait for him to move on."

Gregg shook his head. "It could be a year or more away."

Jack studied the man before him, dimly seen in the gloom of the room. A very ordinary-looking man . . . He said, "What do you want of me?"

"Information—evidence." Gregg rose and paced the room. "You're in a nice position to gather information. Facts and figures, if possible. Names and dates." He came back to stand with his hands in hip pockets. "What d'you think? Will you work with us? Do you want to think it over?"

Jack smiled. "I like your idealism."

"We don't think of ourselves as idealists. We think we're practical."

"What happens when you collect enough evidence?"

"We'll move in with the United States marshal, maybe with troops, certainly with a district judge and we'll put the entire lot of them behind bars." Gregg snapped his fingers. "That part of it's easy. It's the evidence and facts we need desperately. Collworth will hire the best damn lawyers in the country to defend him."

Jack nodded. He thought of Ned Hilton, wondering why they had not contacted him. Maybe because Hilton was a drinking man. Maybe because Hilton would also serve a term.

Gregg read his mind. "We didn't go to the town marshal for a reason. We think he is mixed in with Collworth too deeply and he drinks too much."

"You already know a good deal about the town."

"Of course." Gregg smiled again, his teeth a pale sheen in the darkened room. "You're not the only one working for us in Eagle Rock."

"I see." Jack sniffed the cigarette. "Are your backers cattlemen?"

Gregg shook his head. "Mining interests."

"Collworth has money in several mines—or so I'm told."

"That's true. In a very small way." Gregg took a turn about the room and stood at a window as several riders passed outside in the street. A heavily loaded wagon rumbled by. He came back and sat down. "I am posing as a whiskey drummer —I actually take orders. I will come through Eagle Rock about once a month. We'll arrange to talk then, but in the meantime I'll give you a few names and addresses. You can write to them, send whatever you think is appropriate, and it'll come to me."

Jack fished for a match and chewed it. "Who are you, exactly?"

"I'm an attorney, working for my client. I'm empowered to pay you one hundred dollars a month for—"

"I don't want the money."

Gregg made a face. "There's an old Spanish saying: Money never comes at the wrong time. Take it, my friend. Bury it in the garden if you wish, for later. I assure you, my clients can afford it."

Jack smiled and shrugged. "Very well." He accepted the gold eagles Gregg counted out on his palm. Now he was a secret agent, actively working against Vance Collworth and Nails.

It made him smile.

• • •

Ki and Carlos returned to the mountains much the same way they had gone, avoiding the town, seeing no one on the trail. They arrived late at night, tired and hungry, and Carmelita hurried to heat up food for them and bring a bottle of wine and glasses.

Jessie rose, hearing the stir, and came into the house as Ramon entered. Carlos told them all that had been accomplished.

Ramon asked, "What did the sheriff promise you?"

"Not much," Carlos admitted. "But now it's all on the record."

"You've had a long ride for very little," Ramon told them. He slapped the pistol at his hip. "We must take care of our own problems. The sheriff cares nothing for us. We are Basques."

He slammed out of the house and they heard him ride away down the slope.

"He is not entirely wrong," Ki said. "Does the Lord not help those who help themselves?"

"I wish the Lord would show up with some angels armed with Winchesters," Carlos grumbled. "We are too few. And they know it."

Carmelita brought them coffee. "Do not blaspheme, my brother. We will do what we must do." She sat at the table next to Ki. Her foot found his and rubbed it. He smiled at her.

Carlos rose and went to the door to look at the sky. He came back to the table. "I will sleep for three hours, then go down and relieve Ramon." He paused at the stair. "If any angels show up, put them to work."

"I will see to it," Carmelita said gravely. She slid onto Ki's lap when her brother had gone.

But in a few moments she got up and pulled at his hand, then led him to a room at the back of the house. "No one will disturb us here."

She slid a bolt on the door and scratched a match to light a single slender candle. Turning, her hands went about his neck. "Now you will not get away from me."

He chuckled, embracing and kissing her. "Who would be fool enough to try?"

She tugged at his shirt and he pulled it off over his head.

He sat on the edge of the narrow bed and she helped him tug off his boots. She began to unfasten her dress as he dropped his jeans on a chair and lay back, watching the delicate way she slipped out of her cotton skirt and opened her blouse, revealing ripe, round breasts.

Crawling onto the bed, she laughed to see him erect and eager for her. She gathered up the shaft with both hands, kneading and kissing it. Then she moved up swiftly, legs scissoring his body.

Ki ran his hand down her naked back and fondled her firm, round bottom. How like velvet her skin was!

She wriggled on him and bit his ear. "Are you going to make me wait forever? Do you think I am made of stone?"

"Forever means different things to different people." He rolled her onto her back as she giggled. Her hands plunged between their bodies immediately and she guided the pulsing shaft . . . and sighed deeply. Her legs tightened about him.

Her head went back and she gasped as if catching her breath. He thrust deeply and the bed rocked beneath them. Her hands moved over his face, then slid to his back, and she moaned softly, kissing his cheeks, arching her back and panting with his thrusts. In a few moments she began to move wildly, jerking and sighing, then drumming her heels on the backs of his legs.

He plunged into her, feeling himself on the edge—then spurting, draining . . . gasping . . . and at last tapering off, holding her close as she sighed and kissed him tenderly.

They slept in each other's arms, and the slender candle never wavered as the hours slipped by, the yellow spear flame enduring . . . till finally it guttered and snuffed out as dawn approached.

★

Chapter 12

Ned Hilton sat at a table near the wall of the Golden Slipper, a bottle in front of him and a tumbler glass in his hand. He was bleary drunk.

It was the only way he knew to keep the images away—he thought of them as goblins; they came after him in his sleep, roaring and screaming, tearing at his flesh till he woke, soaked with perspiration and shouting, flailing his arms to keep them off him.

The nightmares never stopped. It was seldom that he could sleep and not have them beat on his soul, tormenting him. The only way he had found was to go to sleep dead drunk.

He would be sick and miserable in the morning, but the horrors had not visited him in the night. Though he sometimes wondered which was worse, the spectres of his dreams or the body-wracking sickness.

And yet, drunk as he was, he knew how others looked at him. He was the town marshal . . . and he knew he had lost everyone's respect. But they didn't know about his terrible dreams. And he could not tell them. Nails would kill him if he talked.

He had begged Nails to let him go away, take the next stage out of town, but Nails had refused. "We like you just as you are," Nails had said in his silky voice, smiling. Oh, how Nails smiled. "Get out of here, Hilton." And he smiled as he said it.

Ned Hilton cried. He felt the tears come and he could not let them see. . . . He put his head down on his arm, lying on the table. How could he get away? He could not think. He was tied hand and foot, bound to this place by Nails. He would be here forever, destined to scream through the horrible dreams. . . .

What were they saying? Two men stood by the table, talking about him. "He's drunk again, stupid drunk. Why the hell does Nails keep him around?"

Ned heard the other say, "Forget him. We've got to join the others and get up to the mountain. It's five miles to the gorge."

They walked away.

Ned blinked through the tears. The gorge. He knew where the gorge was. It was the beginning of a trail into the mountains where the Basques lived.

Basques. They had a damn pretty daughter. . . .

An image of old Fernando Diaz drifted into his mind. Nails wanted to charge him with murder. Nails hated the Basques. . . . But Ned couldn't remember why. Men were going to the gorge. Join others. Maybe go after old Fernando. Nails hated the old man.

Ned rubbed his eyes on his sleeve. It was late at night, he was sure of that. Men going to the gorge late at night?

He sat back and blinked at the room. Lights. Fuzzy, blurry lights. Men moving here and there. Noise and music. He tried to get up and couldn't.

Jesus! He had to get up. Goddamn table in his way. He pushed at it, scraping it away. He managed to stand, pushing against the wall. Damn! he was dizzy. He kept still till it went away. Then he headed for the door.

Someone called to him. A few men laughed. A foot tripped him and he fell headlong, taking a chair down with him. More laughter.

It took him an eon to get up again. Someone helped him

and he mumbled thanks. He got to the door and half fell outside into the night. It was cool, and a breeze felt good on his face. Leaning on the building, he blurred at the street. Where was his horse? Oh, in the stable, a block away.

He headed for it, feeling his way along the building. When the boardwalk ended he fell into the street, tasting dirt. He sat there a bit, getting his breath back. Then he pulled himself up, a little easier this time. Which way was the stable?

He decided on the direction and staggered along the street, pausing once to throw up. He wiped his mouth and leaned on a hitchrail to get his breath again. The street was whirling about, but the stable was only a short way away. He could make out the big open double doors.

When he got near he saw someone was sitting outside. Must be Willie, the owner. "'Lo, Willie."

Willie got up. "Christ! You drunker'n a skunk, Ned. Whyn't you go home. Sleep it off."

"Where's m'horse?" Ned staggered inside. Dark as hell. He ran into a post.

Willie came up behind him. "What do you want your hoss for?"

"Gotta go t'the gorge."

"The gorge? At this time o'night?"

"Ged m'goddamn horse, Willie. Nails goin' to the gorge."

Willie stared at him. "All right. You stay ri'here. I'll throw a saddle on 'im."

"All ri'." Ned slid down the post and sat on the ground, head on his chest.

Willie hurried to the back of the stable and woke Jake, the boy who swamped out for him. "You get over to the Slipper and tell Nails that Ned Hilton is goin' to the gorge."

"Tonight?"

"Do like I tell you, dammit!"

Grumbling, Jake hurried away. Willie pulled Ned's saddle off a pole and threw a blanket on Ned's gray and saddled him quickly. If Nails ever found out he knew Ned was going to the gorge and Nails hadn't been told . . . ! Willie shivered. The livery stable was a center of gossip and it was common talk that Nails was going after the Basques soon. If this was the night . . . Willie shivered again.

He led the horse out and helped Ned to his feet. "You figger you can stay on the hoss?"

"'Course I can. Hep me up." Ned grabbed the horn with both hands. Willie shoved and Ned nearly fell off the other side, but he managed to hold on, swaying.

He walked the gray out to the street and halted, uncertain which way to go. It took him a while to decide because for a moment or two he forgot what he was about. Then he remembered, and headed to the right.

He was going to warn the Basques that Nails was sending men into the mountains. Goddamn Nails. He hated him. He wasn't that crazy about the Basques, but he hated Nails.

When he tried to move faster than a walk, he nearly fell off sideways. It was hard enough to stay on when the gray walked.

It was dark as the inside of a lizard when he left the town behind. And he easily got lost. He could not find the gorge. Several times he went to sleep and woke, grabbing the horn, surprised to find himself on a horse.

The gray took the main road out of town, plodding along steadily while Ned bleared at the passing trees, wondering where he was. Wondering what he was doing here.

When he remembered, he halted the horse and thought about it. The mountain where the Basques lived was off to the left. He was positive of that. But where the trail was, he had no idea, and it was dark. Jesus! it was dark . . . despite the moon.

He was about to turn the horse to the left when he heard hoofbeats approaching. He halted and stared at them stupidly. Three men came up to him and reined in. One said, "Where you goin', Ned?"

"That you, Tim?" Was it Tim Hickson? Tim had a broken arm.

"Yeah, it's me. Where you goin', Ned?"

"Goin' back t'town."

"Oh? I thought you were goin' to the gorge."

Ned shook his head. "Can' find it."

"What you want to find it for?" Hickson's tone was ominous.

Ned shook his head. He looked at them blearily, his slack

jaw open. He shouldn't be talking about the gorge. He touched his spurs to the gray's flank. "Goin' home."

But one of the men grabbed his reins, halting the horse. Hickson said, "You ain't goin' nowhere, Ned." He drew his revolver and fired.

Ned gasped. He fell backward with the slam of the heavy bullet and hit the ground as the horse skittered. He sprawled facedown in the dirt and Hickson fired again, into the back of his head.

In the office of the Slipper, Hickson reported to Nails. "Ned was goin' to the gorge, all right. The dumb sonofabitch was so drunk he told us."

"What'd you do?"

"Dumped the body into the brush. Harry took 'is horse out to his place in the flats. Nobody'll find it there."

Nails nodded. "Who'd you take with you?"

"Harry and his cousin, Joe."

"All right. Go back. You take a buckboard out there with both of them and you bury the body. I want it nice and deep . . . not close to the road either."

Hickson nodded. "All right."

"What'd you take off'n the body?"

"Nothing."

"You take his pistol?"

Hickson hesitated. "Maybe Joe did."

Nails pointed his finger and his soft voice had an edge to it. "You bury that pistol with him. Don't you take no rings or nothing. What about his saddle . . . it got any marks on it?"

"I dunno."

"You find out and come back t'me. If it got marks, I want it destroyed. Hear?"

Hickson nodded and went out. Jesus, Nails was thorough. Joe wasn't going to like it about the pistol. . . .

★

Chapter 13

Ramon had his seven men spaced out along the mountain, lower down, watching the trails, including the one that winded past the dry stream into the gorge. He did not pay special attention to the gorge, even though it had a path, because that particular area was a very poor one for an attack. It had little cover, and the path was so steep in places that anyone using it would make considerable noise.

Of course townsmen might not know that. . . .

Ramon and his volunteers had been patrolling for months, ever since the first sheep-killings. Ramon himself kept on the move constantly, moving from one outpost to the next, sharing coffee, making sure every man was alert. Eight men were really not enough to watch the entire area.

So far they had caught no one killing sheep. The killing had been done silently, with knives. The killers had doubtless come on foot, shadows in the dark.

An attack on the Basque homes was not anticipated. The sheep killers doubtless wanted to drive out the Basques; but to *murder* everyone? Even Ramon did not think it a possibility or something to guard against.

Fernando and his friends had come from the old country, but Ramon, his brother and sister, and the people their age had played in the mountains all their lives and had devised games using bird calls as signals as the Indians did. These came in handy to the guards.

When Ramon heard the peculiar owl hoots from the direction of the gorge, he rode that way at once. "What is it?"

A dozen men had passed, the guard told him, and were heading for the tiny Basque settlement, seven miles away. "They are taking the gorge trail."

Ramon sent him for the others. They would come together at a particular ridge where the gorge trail crossed it. Ramon rode for the ridge, heart pounding. So they had come at last! But if his men arrived in time they would set an ambush. They *must* be enemies. Why else would they come at night, unannounced?

Three men showed up at once only a few moments after he had arrived himself. Ramon placed them on the ridge, looking down the path. "Wait till I tell you to fire!"

He listened, and in a few minutes he could hear the jingling of equipment and the hoofs of a number of horses striking rock as they climbed the steeply rising trail. Another man, the youngest of his crew, showed up and Ramon placed him behind a tree as the first horseman appeared in the shadows.

Instantly the youth fired. Ramon swore, and suddenly everyone was firing! Ramon dropped to the ground and lead whined over him, rapping into trees with wicked sounds. He emptied his pistol at the flashes and rolled to his left, reloading quickly.

A horse screamed and went down, legs threshing. Men were shouting in the brush below the ridge. Ramon got to his feet and ran forward a few yards. The invaders had been taken by surprise and halted in thier tracks—were they falling back?

But after a few moments they must know that only a few guns faced them.

At the house, Ki heard the sudden distant shots and rushed outside. Jessica joined him in a moment. "What is it?"

"I don't know—but I think Ramon's in a fight!" Ki ran back inside, picked a Winchester off a stand, and levered the breech open; it was loaded. Shoving a box of shells into a pocket, he hurried back outside.

"I'm going down there. You stay here in case they get by us. Better find Carmelita."

"I'm here." Carmelita spoke from the doorway, a rifle in her hands.

Ki said, "They may try to set fire to the houses."

"We'll be ready for them."

Ki nodded and ran, heading for the sound of firing. It was a long way off, but sound traveled on a still night. The shots were like corn popping in a pan. He hoped there was only one bunch of them; if they had attacked from two directions it was likely they would burn out the houses.

But Jessica was a holy terror in a fight, and Carmelita had said she could shoot. Maybe the houses would go, but the women would get some of the attackers first.

A few bullets whined overhead—strays. The sounds died away as he approached. Then they started again in bursts of pistol fire.

He came to a rocky area and paused to get his bearings. Most of the firing was directly in front, along the slope of the mountain. Several bullets cut through the trees above him, showering him with twigs.

A bullet spanged off a rock nearby and Ki ducked down, cradling the rifle as he crawled forward. Maybe the invaders were holed up in the rocks.

The moon was bright; but it provided very little light, and none at all in the deep shadows. Someone was yelling but he could not make out the words. A riderless horse burst from the underbrush and galloped past him, eyes wild.

Then for a moment the firing stopped and Ki lay still, listening. Was that movement in front of him?

He moved forward silently, keeping to the deep shadows, and came to a rock formation, like giant teeth in the gloom. He moved around it as the firing came again in hard bursts. He could hear someone swearing.

Then, as he rounded a jumble of rocks, he saw Ramon. The Basque was lying by a fallen tree, reloading his pistol. As Ki watched, Ramon lifted his head, looking over the tree, then ducked again.

And just beyond him a man came into view, aiming a rifle at the spot where Ramon had just been. When Ramon lifted his head again—

Ki slowly lifted the Winchester, squeezing the trigger.

Ramon turned his head and saw Ki just as he fired. The bullet nearly scraped the fallen tree and the man with the rifle disappeared. The rifle clattered on the rocks and Ramon smiled.

When the rifle fire slackened and died away, the invaders had retreated. They had left four bodies in the brush. One horse was dead.

Of Ramon's men, two were wounded and one dead. It had been a nasty fight in the dark.

"Who were they?" Ki asked.

"They came from the town." Ramon shrugged. "I think they must be Collworth's men. When the sun comes up we will see if anyone recognizes the dead ones."

One of his men had followed the invaders down the mountain and reported later that all had returned to the town, several on foot.

"Now they know we are alert," Ramon said with satisfaction.

When they were alone, Ramon put his arm about Ki's shoulders. "And you, my friend, I am forever in your debt."

Nails was disgusted and did not hide it. A dozen men had not been able to reach the Basque settlement. "Not even in the middle of the goddamn night! Did you go with torches? Did somebody blow a damned bugle to wake them all up?"

"They were waiting for us," a man complained.

"How could they know you were coming?"

"They were there," the man grumbled.

Nails swore and sent them all away. Was he surrounded by bumblers? Did they wish him to believe that all the Basques were twelve feet tall?

He was still in a foul mood when Hickson returned and rapped on his office door.

Hickson reported, "All right, he's buried, and I looked at the saddle. It's a cheap one without no marks. Nobody could swear it was Hilton's. They must be a hunnerd like it in the county."

Nails nodded. He let out his breath. Somebody was doing something right. He leaned back in his chair and struck a match, lighting his cigar. He gazed at Hickson through the smoke. "How's your arm?"

"All right. Healing good, the doc says. Be good as new in a week'r so."

"You feel up to taking over the town marshal's job?"

"Sure." Hickson grinned. Then he frowned. "How about Jack English?"

"What about him? He'll take orders."

Hickson shrugged.

Nails said, "I got to have a man I can trust. I'm not sure of Jack. He's too goddamn independent—which is why he ain't going to be marshal. If you can't get along with him, then you fire him. Hear?"

"I got it." Hickson nodded. He reached in his pocket. "Ned had eleven dollars on him."

Nails waved the cigar. "You keep it."

Hickson smiled and went out.

The disappearance of Ned Hilton caused a ripple in the town. Despite his being a drunk, many liked him and asked about him. They came to Jack English, who had no idea.

"Ned didn't tell me anything. The last time anybody saw him was at the Slipper. They tell me he was dead drunk."

"That's right." A lot of people had seen him flopped over the table. One or two said he'd lurched out to the street later. He might have crawled in a hole somewhere. Drunks did crazy things.

Jack ambled over to the livery. If Ned had gone anywhere he must have taken his horse. How could you go anywhere at all without a horse? Old Willie was up and pitching hay. Jack asked him if Ned had come into the stable for his nag, and Willie said he had.

"Drunker'n two hunnerd skunks too."

"He got on his horse? Where'd he go?"

Willie shook his head. "I didn't foller 'im. I saddled the gray and went on back and hit the hay. None o' my business whur he went."

Jack nodded. "Thanks."

He went out to the street and stood in a patch of shade, rolling a cigarette. What old Willie had told him didn't ring true. None of Willie's business? Very damned strange. Willie was the biggest gossip in six counties . . . liked to hear everything. It was not like him to saddle Ned's horse and let him ride off drunk and not ask him where he was going.

He could go back and probably shake it out of the old man pretty easy, but somebody—like Nails—was sure to want to know why. But more than that, if Will didn't want him to know, maybe it was important.

He lit the brown cigarette and puffed absently. What was the most important thing in Eagle Rock? Vance Collworth's business. Managed by Nails.

Did Ned's sudden disappearance have anything to do with Collworth? Or maybe Nails had sent Ned on a mission of some kind. No, he wouldn't use a drunk. He flicked ashes into the street.

Had Ned found out something he shouldn't know? Wasn't that the most likely? He might have stumbled into something and said too much to Nails. When he was drunk, Ned would run off at the mouth.

Maybe Nails had gotten rid of him—permanently. Did old Willie know it?

Jack puffed on the cigarette, looked at it, and flipped it into the street. Ned had taken to drink more and more of late. Jack knew there was something on the man's mind, but hadn't pressed him. It could have been any of a number of things . . . maybe money. He knew that Ned was supporting a child or two somewhere. It could have been that. He knew that Ned had been very unhappy about some of the things Nails had required him to do, and had spoken a few times about the way Nails used him.

Sighing, Jack walked to the office and eased himself into Ned's chair. The desk wasn't locked, and he glanced through the drawers finding nothing of interest.

Well, maybe Ned would turn up in the morning, having slept off a drunk somewhere.

• • •

But he did not. In the morning Tim Hickson showed up and handed Jack a surprise. Hickson said he'd been appointed town marshal by Nails.

"I'll be damned." Jack smiled, staring at the man. Hickson's arm was no longer in a sling, but it was bandaged. He stood and offered his hand. Hickson shook it and glanced around the office. Two desks and chairs, a bench, and rifles in a rack to one side.

"Which is my desk?"

"That one," Jack pointed. "It was Ned's anyway. You can have either one, of course."

Hickson went over and sat behind it.

Jack pulled out the makin's and deftly rolled a cigarette. Hickson here as marshal? Hadn't Nails made a big mistake? His appointment of Hickson showed—didn't it?—that he knew what had happened to Ned. So Nails knew that Ned wasn't coming back. Very interesting.

But Nails should have waited a day or two, or a week at least.

So Ned Hilton was dead. Jack was suddenly sure of it. And probably Tim Hickson knew it too. Jack puffed the cigarette. Maybe Hickson had helped him along to the Pearly Gates. Hickson had a rep as a hard case.

Mumbling something about making rounds, Jack got out of the office. A man had to have a chance to think. Did he want to remain on as deputy to Hickson? Maybe he should sleep on it. His first impression was unfavorable.

That morning Jack had heard about the midnight raid on the Basques because four men of the town were dead as a result, and three had light wounds that Doc Hamblin had treated.

Jack went from the office to the undertaker's place, and asked to see the deceased. The undertaker was out somewhere but his assistant, a red-haired man who sniffed continually, let him in. Jack recognized all of them, knew them by sight, though names did not come to him. All of them had worked for Nails in one capacity or other. He wondered how much Nails had paid them to be part of the army.

He hoped they had made wills. They were a sad-looking bunch laid out on the long tables. Red Hair drew sheets over the faces when Jack backed away.

Jack went from there to the nearest saloon and ordered beer. All around him the talk was about the raid. About a dozen men had gone into the mountains; the speculation at the bar was that they'd gone to burn out the Basque settlement. What else?

But they had never reached it. They had been ambushed and cut up. They had managed to bring out the dead, and those who survived had sworn they'd never go back.

No one knew the cost to the Basques but it was generally assumed they had lost a few men too.

When Jack asked one particular question, no one knew the answer. Jack asked, "Why'd they go up there anyhow?"

Someone said, "Because they was paid to."

Someone else asked, "Who paid 'em?"

Even the men who had received the pay didn't know. One of those lying on the undertaker's metal-lined table had done the paying.

Jack thought the money had probably come from Nails. But he didn't say so.

He made a note of it all for Homer Gregg.

★

Chapter 14

Ramon and Carlos, with nine men from the settlement, some of them very young, dug rifle pits along the mountain trails. These were carefully placed and concealed. One of the lessons learned in the War Between the States was that one man in a rifle pit, or dug in, was worth three in the open.

These pits were manned day and night, and a signal system was agreed upon. Three quickly spaced shots meant extreme emergency. Ramon instructed them, "Don't fire in the air. Fire at *them*. We'll hear the shots."

Jessica, Ki, Carlos, and Ramon, with Carmelita quietly knitting beside them, discussed the night raid. Ramon thought that the fact that a dozen men had come raiding into the mountains was probably the overture.

Jessica thought it might be the opening movement. "There will be more."

Carlos voiced it for all of them: "What exactly is it they're after?"

"They want you out of here. Out of the mountains," Ki said.

Jessie shook her head. "There's more to it than that."

"What else could it be?" Ramon asked. "They want the land, and to get it they have to push us off."

Carlos said, "But there's plenty of land not taken up by homesteading! The cattlemen are using thousands of acres in the flats. All they own are the waterholes."

"They don't want the flats," Ramon said heatedly.

"Why not?" Jessie asked.

"It has to be the land," Ramon insisted. "It's all we have. They don't want our sheep!"

"Nails and the impostor, Collworth, aren't cattlemen," Jessica said. "So if those two want the land, what will they use it for?"

"Mining," Ki said. "That's all that's left."

"That's right. Mining." Ramon snapped his fingers.

Ki looked around at them. "Didn't you say that someone has been prospecting?"

"Yes," Carlos said. "Someone has."

"Have you investigated the holes they dug?"

Carlos blinked. "No—we haven't. Whoever it was covered up the holes and tried to conceal them. Wouldn't that mean he didn't find anything?"

Carmelita said, "Maybe they found something and wanted us to think that."

Carlos said, "We thought it was because they didn't want us to know they'd been here." He rubbed his cheek. "Maybe they did find something."

Jessica smiled. "There's only one way to find out."

"Vance Collworth" came from Pennsylvania, where he had been a blue-sky salesman, selling what he said was mining stock—without a mine attached. He had beautifully printed, gilt-edged certificates on expensive paper that impressed unsophisticated people, causing them to part with their savings.

His real handle was Thurston Penry and he had spent several years in a state pen after being convicted of child molesting. He was a mild-mannered man on the surface, but was given to uncontrollable rages at odd times.

In the pen he met other con men and discussed with them

other methods of shearing the sheep, to be used when he got out.

On the outside his profession required him to be constantly on the move and often he was but one jump ahead of the law. Once or twice a year, depending on his business luck, he journeyed to St. Louis on the Mississippi where he replenished his stocks of certificates from a certain printer.

He never did business in the city and was not wanted there. Generally in St. Louis he took a month to relax. It was an entire month when he did not have to be continually looking over his shoulder.

In St. Louis, at a hotel gathering, he met Harry Pike, whose friends called him Nails. Nails was recently out of the pen himself. A lawyer had gotten a murder charge reduced to manslaughter, and because of several circumstances, Nails had been released early. He was looking for just such a man as Penry . . . even to his physical characteristics.

Over several suppers and bottles, he revealed a plan to take over the town of Eagle Rock, Colorado—as the first of many such takeovers.

Having nothing to lose, Penry listened, then went along with the scheme. In Eagle Rock he was to impersonate a man called Vance Collworth, who had recently purchased the largest saloon and dance-hall in the town. As Nails outlined it, they would stay in the town for a short time and then move on, because Nails was sure trouble would come.

But when they moved into the town—it did not.

Nails took over the operation of the saloon and the dance hall, fired all the employees and hired new ones. "Vance" stayed in the office. He was a good accountant, and he kept the books. And trouble never appeared—maybe because Nails had a rep as a hard case and had surrounded himself with other gunmen. No one dared cross him.

The operation of the Golden Slipper was very profitable—more than they had figured. Nails stayed very close to the cash, reporting only about two thirds to his partner; he pocketed the rest and often wondered why he needed "Vance." He could hire a bookkeeper for less.

But the thing that ultimately made all the difference in the world was old George Skate. He came wandering into town with a rawboned horse and a black mule with a battered pack, and had asked to see Mr. Collworth.

Why Nails had let the old coot into his office and listened to him, he could not have said later . . . except that it was a hunch. He'd bought the old man a beer and lunch and gave him an ear for an hour—then he had actually grubstaked Skate. Nails had never done such a thing before in his life; he was a taker, not a giver.

But old George Skate went up into the mountains, dodging the Basques, digging in odd places—and found a vein of silver a yard wide.

Of course, it was on Basque-owned property.

George Skate didn't know this, and Nails did not tell him. Skate had made a detailed map for Nails, one that a child could follow, and then unfortunately George had met with an accident late at night and never regained consciousness.

Nails sold the horse and mule and all Skate's tools to pay for a very nice funeral.

Carlos and two men went looking for the prospector's holes, and dug each one up. They located seven holes altogether. The last two were very close together, under a cliff face, and each was startling.

"A huge vein of silver!" Carlos told them. They were assembled in the main room of the house. "No wonder someone wants this land!"

The others were astonished. "There has never been any silver found on this side of the mountain!" Carmelita exclaimed.

"Until now."

"But I mean, why would anyone even come to look for it?"

"Prospectors look everywhere. Maybe one didn't know there was no silver here—so he found it. One just happened to drift along our mountain, digging holes."

"And then he covered them up," Jessie said musingly. "I wonder who he reported to."

Ramon grunted. "He reported to Nails. That's why Nails sent his killers here. And he'll do it again till he pushes us off or kills all of us."

Ki asked, "Does Nails have the money to buy men to fight

us? Four have been killed already. Are more men going to get into that buzz saw for a few dollars?"

"I agree. Death is very permanent," Carmelita said.

Carlos sighed. "I think he will find the men. Maybe bring them in from somewhere else. A bullet always hits the other person, doesn't it?"

"What if we move farther into the mountains?" Carmelita said softly. "We could make it more difficult for them to reach us. And easier for us to reach them."

"I don't like it," Ramon objected.

"It may be a good idea," Carlos said approvingly. "It would save us much worry about our homes."

"We have always lived here," Ramon said. "I don't want to give up our homes to that bastard."

"There is one other thing," Ki said gently, "something that might save us all a lot of trouble."

Ramon looked at him. "What's that?"

"We could hit at the core of the trouble. Get rid of him and the problem might easily go away."

Ramon smiled. "You mean Nails."

"Yes. Nails."

Chapter 15

"Killing Nails is a noble thought, amigo," Ramon said. "But it may not be very practical. He surrounds himself with guns."

"Does he never go outside the saloon?"

Carlos shrugged. "We do not know."

"Then we must find out."

Carmelita shook her head. "That will be very dangerous. They know us all by sight, I am sure."

Ki smiled. "In the dark all cats are alike."

"He is more than a cat," Jessie said. "So you are going into the town?"

Ki nodded.

Ramon said, "I will go with you."

"No. You are needed here. They may come back at any time."

"That is true," Carlos said. "We cannot spare you."

Ramon scowled, but he did not press the point.

Ki made his preparations and got several hours' sleep, rising an hour before midnight. Jessica was awake to see him off. They had parted often in the past, for short periods, but each time was like the last, and none was easy. It was foolish to say "be careful," and she did not. He merely smiled and was gone in the gloom.

Ramon provided him with a guide to show the quickest way to the town's outskirts. The guide left him there with a wave of his hand. Ki paused and gazed at the town; there were but few lanterns burning and few horses along the street. The town was asleep. It was a weeknight, after all.

He left the horse tied between two buildings and moved into the town slowly, watchfully. The Slipper was in the center of town and still lighted . . . but maybe the lights burned all night. He crossed the wide street and halted again to watch and listen. Nothing moved; no one was sitting in any of the chairs along the street or on the benches. He could see no one in any of the doorways.

A light was on in the marshal's office, but that probably burned all night too. He went to the same side of the street as the Slipper and approached it warily. A wagon sat in front of the door, without a team. The Slipper door was closed and probably locked.

Ki went back till he found a space between buildings, and then went through to the back of the row. There were more wagons here, and some stables and privies, and it was much darker. The back door to the Slipper was large—a double door, locked with a chain. He fingered it. No one would get through it without blasting powder.

Stepping back, he looked up at the windows on the second floor. Did Collworth or Nails sleep in the building? There were a number of girls who worked the saloon and dance-hall; maybe some of them slept there where they did business.

Too many maybes.

One of the windows was open slightly. Ki frowned at it, debating with himself. What could he gain by going inside? The answer: how would he know without going?

A logical answer, he thought.

The Slipper was not a really marvelous construction job; it had probably been built by odd-lot carpenters with what lumber was available. It was stout enough but roughly finished. It was child's play to climb up to the second floor window and push it up. He slid inside and found himself in an office. It was a small room, certainly not Vance Collworth's office; maybe his assistant's.

A door was standing open. Ki crossed the room and looked into a hall. As he stood by the door he could hear the murmur of voices. To his left was a partly open door from which light streamed. The room from which it came was on the side of the building, which was why he had not seen the light from the alley.

There were other doors along the hall, but all were closed. If he moved along the hall he might overhear what was being said, but if one of them looked into the hall, there would be fireworks. He had nowhere to hide.

He debated for only a moment. It was worth a chance. He stepped into the hall and ducked back quickly. Someone came to the other door and opened it wide. Ki saw him clearly. It was Nails. Nails said goodnight to someone inside, then turned and went along the hall in the other direction, out of Ki's sight.

The other man, whoever he was, came to the door, closed it, and locked it. The hall was suddenly very dark.

Softly, Ki said, "Damn." The man inside the room was undoubtedly Collworth. Had he missed an important conversation? There was no way of knowing.

He went back to the window and let himself out, pulling the window down so it was barely open. He might need it again.

He had just reached the ground again and taken a single step when a voice said, "Izzat you, Bert? What the hell you doin' back here?"

"I'm going," Ki said.

There was a pause and the voice said, "You ain't Bert!"

Ki had identified the speaker; he stood in the deep shadow of a shed perhaps ten feet away. So Nails had posted guards, and one of them had come awake at an awkward time.

The voice said, "Come out where I kin see you."

"All right," Ki said in an amiable tone. He slid behind a pile of boxes, crouched down and crawled to a privy. He faced only one man; the man called Bert was probably out on the street.

He heard the man swear, then a gunshot sounded and

splinters flew from one of the boxes behind him.

Another shot. Ki heard it rap into the side of the privy just over his head. The shots would bring men running. . . . Ki kept the privy between him and the shooter. He ducked behind a row of sheds as the man fired again. This time the shot went into the air, and Ki smiled. The man had lost him.

He crossed the alley silently, slid over a low fence, and ran along the end of a stable, around a corral where several mules stared at him, and made his way back to his horse.

Mounting, he sat in the saddle for a minute listening to the sounds. Men were calling; the town was roused by the shooting and Ki laughed to himself. Someone would get kicked in the ass for raising all the ruckus when no interloper was found.

He went back to the mountain, whistling a tune under his breath.

Jack English had no illusions about Nails. When Tim Hickson was put into Ned's job as town marshal, the writing was on the wall. His time as deputy was getting short. He knew that Nails suspected him of not being loyal.

Loyal to Nails? The idea was laughable.

When he was sure Ned was not coming back, he had gone to Ned's boardinghouse and sorted through Ned's belongings, looking for a relative's name and address. He found the names of Ned's two daughters, and their addresses, but he also found a notebook. Ned had kept a kind of diary. Much of it was accounts, money earned and money spent. But a good half was notations about his job and opinions about his employers.

Jack whistled, reading them. Ned called Nails and Collworth both the worst kind of crooks, and he enumerated some of the things Nails had required of him.

There were names and dates, exactly what Homer Gregg had asked him to find. Jack put the notebook in his pocket. Ned hadn't owned much of any value. There was nothing to send to his daughters but a silver watch and a few letters. Not much satisfaction in them.

When he returned to the office, Tim Hickson was there, in a bad mood, wearing a star on his shirt. "Where you been?"

"Looking at the town."

"I'll tell you when to look at the goddamn town."

"All right," Jack said mildly. "I'm just doing what I've always done. What're your orders, sir?"

"You're a smart-mouth, aren't you?"

Jack smiled. "Smart enough to know a jackass like you when I see one."

Hickson jumped up and charged Jack, his eyes wild. Jack easily knocked him aside and pushed him into a chair. "Don't hurt your arm, Timmy."

Hickson went for his gun and Jack kicked it out of his hand. It slammed against the wall and skittered under a desk.

"You're fired!" Hickson yelled. "Git the hell outta this office!"

"I'm fired?"

"You're damn right you are!"

"In that case—" Jack hit him solidly on the jaw. Hickson went over backward, sprawling on the floor with the chair atop him.

Jack removed the badge from his cartridge belt and pinned it to Hickson's shirt. He cleaned out his desk and left the office. Hickson was still out cold.

He walked up the street to the Alamo Saloon, across from the Golden Slipper, and sat at a table, his back to the wall. There was a boy cleaning the brass cuspidors, and Jack gave him a dime to take a message across the street.

"Tell Nails I'm here. Tell 'im also that he's a piece of dogshit."

The lad stared at him with eyes round as pie tins.

"Go on," Jack urged.

The boy ran out and Jack placed his six-gun on the table in front of him and yelled for beer.

★

Chapter 16

One of Ramon's men was named Nick Sanchez, a youth of twenty-six. He was doubly important because his sister, Maria, was married to Elmer Canfield, one of the two grocers in Eagle Rock.

Canfield was a good man, well liked by the miners he traded with. His store did a steady business—not enough to attract Nails's eye, but enough to allow the Canfields to put something by.

The Canfields had a son, Joseph, who was fifteen.

Twice a month, long after the store was closed for the night, Elmer and Maria loaded a light wagon with supplies and covered it with a canvas tarpaulin. Young Joseph would drive it to a mountain path, where it was met by Nick. The supplies were transferred and Joseph would drive back and put the horse in the corral.

Long before, Ramon and his father, when they came to the post office each week, had let it be known that they received their supplies from across the mountain to the east. Apparently Nails believed the story and had never looked into it. So young Joseph continued to deliver to the Basques, under Nails's nose, without detection.

Possibly a more elaborate plan would have caused talk at least, or had someone poking into it. Maria took pains to call herself Mary, and no one in the town knew of her Basque beginnings.

Each week Carlos took supplies to his father and mother in their hideaway home, and the next time that Carlos went, Jessica accompanied him with the pack mule plodding along behind.

The hideaway was in a canyon where a spring burbled out of the ground and fed a tiny patch of grass before disappearing again into the earth. The house was more than a hut: a solid log-built house that backed up to the hillside and was partly dug in, with a log roof several feet thick on which grew a profusion of wild plants and a small tree. From above, Carlos told her, the house was almost invisible.

They were expected. Fernando, completely well again and spry, came out to greet them, bowing in courtly fashion to Jessie. "How nice of you to come to see us."

Carlos said, "She wouldn't stay away."

"And why should she?" Fernando took her arm and they went inside.

His wife, Dolores, served them wine at once, asking for news. "We have heard nothing . . ."

"For a week," Fernando said.

Carlos told them that everything was quiet—not wanting to alarm his mother. Jessie, watching the older Diaz, thought he was not taken in, though he said nothing.

Nothing, that is, until they were about to leave. Then he walked down the path a little way with them, chatting with Jessie. And when they turned and the house was out of sight, he asked Carlos, "What has happened? Has Collworth attacked you?"

"Yes, we think so, Father. We are not positive it is Collworth."

"Have you found a reason?"

"Yes," Jessie said. "Silver."

Diaz was astonished. "Silver?"

Carlos told him about the prospector's holes, and what they had discovered.

Diaz was silent for several moments. "It means nothing but trouble. What about the law?"

"I have gone to the sheriff, with Ki. The sheriff will not help us . . . but he does not know about the silver. That may change everything."

"Perhaps for the better," Jessie said.

Diaz sighed, shaking his head. "I wish there were no silver. . . . "

Jack English sat for two hours, sipping beer, talking with hangers-on. They all said the same thing. Nails himself would not show . . . but Jack knew that, deep down.

He also had a very good idea what Nails would do—if he did anything. He might ignore the threat. But if he did not, he would probably send two men, one to the front door and one to the back. If they struck at him at the same time, they would probably win. And off he would go to Boot Hill.

So he sat in the middle of the room, his back to the wall, where he could watch both doors.

One time, years ago, he had been in a saloon where a tinhorn was steadily fleecing several cowhands. To Jack's practiced eye, the gambler was dealing honestly—he did not have to cheat to win over clumsy players. But one of the cowhands flew into a rage at a lost pot and clawed for his gun.

The tinhorn shot him in the belly. His gun never got above the table.

Jack had a second gun in his lap with the butt only inches from his right hand and already pointed at the front door.

When a man looked into the room but did not come in, Jack knew they had arrived. The man at the front had the best chance at him, he thought. The man coming in the back door cast a shadow on the wall—he had noticed the shadow when several customers had gone out the back way. The shadow would tell him the man was approaching.

He slid his fingers around the butt of the pistol in his lap and cocked it.

He had two or three minutes to think about it; then the man came in the front with a rifle pointed at him. Jack shot him twice, and the rifle-shot splintered the ceiling. The man fell backwards into the street.

With his left hand he fired, too soon, at the man on his right. The man's answering shot seared his arm, but Jack's second shot hit his assailant in the throat. Jack shot him again before he reached the floor, spraying the wall with brains. Then he stood up and pulled off his coat. His arm was bloody.

One of the bartenders, a skinny type named Harry, came running and cut away the sleeve. He daubed it with water. "Hell, it's only a scratch, Jack. Didn't come nowhere near the bone. You be fine in a couple days."

"It stings," Jack said, frowning at it. "Did you know those fellers?"

"One. Seen him b'fore, anyways. The one who come in the back. Never saw the one out front—didn't get a good look at him. That was nice shootin', Jack."

"Thanks." He gritted his teeth as Harry bound up the wound. "Here, buy the house a drink." He put down a coin.

"What you goin' do now, Jack?"

Jack looked at the front window. "Getting dark out. My horse's in back. Think I'll hit the trail." He watched two men drag the body out to the front; they laid both bodies on the sidewalk, waiting for the undertaker.

Reloading the pistols, Jack had a drink and thought about his next move. He couldn't stay in town; Nails was sure to hunt him down if he did. There was only one place to go, unless he took the stage. He'd ride to the Basque settlement and talk to them . . . now that they were both enemies of Nails's.

He got up, waved to Harry, and went out tugging on his coat. He rode straight across the weedy fields from the back of the saloon, the shadows long and rippling in front of the horse. The sun was almost gone. When he came to the edge of the trees he halted and gazed around. No one was coming after him. It would take a while to get a pursuit together—if Nails wanted him that bad.

He turned south and headed for the mountains.

It was still light when he reached the foothills. Too bad Nails had sent those two men instead of coming himself. He had missed all the excitement.

The trail was well defined. He walked the horse, then halted as he went around a curve. Three men faced him, all with rifles across their thighs. One asked, "Where you going?"

"I'm Jack English. Come to pay a visit." He saw them murmur among themselves, then one turned and loped away. Another said, "We wait."

Jack nodded. In about fifteen minutes Ramon showed up.

"Hello, Jack. You on official business?"

"Hell, no. I've been fired."

Ramon came closer, noticing the torn sleeve. "You been shot?"

"Had a little fracas, yes. It's only a scratch. Nails wanted me in a box."

Ramon made a face. "Nails came after you?"

"No, he sent a couple of men. You want my guns?"

"No. You're our friend, aren't you?"

"I am. Especially today." Jack smiled. "Guess I'm a saddle bum."

"Come to the house." Ramon turned his horse. "They'll be glad to see you."

They all seemed delighted to see him. Jessica noticed the blood on his coat. "Are you hurt?"

"Just a scratch." He took the coat off gingerly and she examined the wound after removing Harry's crude bandage.

"It doesn't look bad . . ." She pointed to a chair. "You sit there. I'll get some hot water."

He told them how it had happened, and Carlos laughed. "Too bad Nails didn't come after you himself."

Ki said, "That was a crazy thing to do, Jack. What if Nails had sent half a dozen men?"

Jack grinned. "The world will flounder and sink on 'what ifs.' He didn't send them. That's the main thing."

Jessie returned with a pan of water and washed the wound carefully, then applied a yellow salve that Carmelita gave her. She bandaged the wound deftly and he thanked her with a kiss on the cheek.

Chapter 17

Nails was given to periods of rage mixed with frustration. Too many of the men he hired or dealt with were incompetents or idiots. Either they would not do as he expected, or they could not.

It was inconceivable, for instance, that Jack English could sit in the saloon across the street, defying him for hours. "Come and get me," Jack had been saying.

He was sore tempted to go himself, but Jack was uncommonly good with a six-gun—so everyone told him—and death was so very lasting and immutable. One lucky bullet could end all his dreams and plans.

So he sent two men and gave them the plan. "Hit him together, at the same time from two directions. He cannot see you both then, and he will lose."

But he had not. And Jack had ridden away unscathed.

Nails sat in his office with a bottle. He was not a drinking man, but now and then the liquor soothed him. His rage was so often just under the surface—but everyone did not recognize that fact.

One of those was Thurston Penry, who now called himself

Collworth. Penry considered himself a partner, but he was not aware of everything Nails did.

But he became aware of one thing. Unfortunately his timing was poor. He learned that Nails was pocketing cash from the saloon. And he learned it the day that Jack English had defied Nails. It was not the best day to confront Nails. But he had not known that, either.

He went to Nails's office that night when everyone in the offices upstairs had gone home. The girls and their customers were in another part of the building. He demanded an accounting.

Nails glared at him. "We can talk about that later."

"I want to know now. How much have you cheated me?"

"You sonofabitch!" Nails yelled. "Get out of here!"

Penry pounded a desk. "I got a right!"

"The hell you have," Nails said. He pulled a pistol and shot Penry three times in the chest.

Penry's eyes became round for an instant, and he fell backward across another desk and rolled heavily to the floor, facedown. Powder smoke swirled in the little room.

"Shit!" Nails said aloud. He got up and looked down at the body. Now he'd have to get rid of it. And best do it himself. He looked at the window. It was closed. He went to the hall door to listen, but could hear nothing untoward. Probably the shots hadn't been heard downstairs. Shots in the town weren't that unusual anyway.

He got a bottle out of the desk and poured into a glass. Penry had pushed him just a little too far, the stupid bastard. Well, he'd been thinking of getting rid of him anyhow. Not exactly this way, but this would do. He drank the liquor down and put the bottle away. Best get about it.

He knew exactly what he had to do.

He went down the hall to Penry's office, a much larger one than his, with shelves full of papers and books, two cabinets of papers and invoices . . . lots of paper. Penry had been fond of records.

Nails spent half an hour tidying up Penry's desk. He wanted it to look as if Penry had put everything away before going on a trip.

That done, he took Penry's coat from behind the door and

went back to his own office. He went downstairs to a storage room and found a length of rope. The saloon was closing up; he did not enter it. Upstairs again, he sat and smoked a cigar, waiting for the last customers to leave. Things would be different without Penry. He'd have to get another bookkeeper, but that shouldn't be any problem. He'd send to Kimberly to the weekly there and advertise for one.

When the saloon downstairs was finally closed and locked, Nails tied the rope around the body, opened the window and lowered it to the ground, tossing the coat after it. Then he went down and out the back door. There was a buckboard in the stable. He carried the body and tossed it in with the coat and covered it with a tarpaulin. He hunted down a shovel and put that in also.

He thought he heard a sound from outside. He pulled his pistol and slipped out into the dark, but no one was there. His nerves were taut.

Backing a horse into the shafts, he hooked up and opened the stable door. He led the horse and wagon through, locked the door, and drove out of town.

He went north, toward the flats, and drove steadily for an hour. When he halted, the silence was eerie, a thousand miles deep. Off to his right were huge leaning rocks. He drove the wagon off the rutted trail and halted near the rocks.

With the shovel, he dug a four-foot-deep grave. Four feet was plenty deep enough for Penry. He rolled the body in, dropping in the coat, and shoveled the earth back, tramping it down as he went. Nobody would ever find him out here. He scattered the earth around instead of mounding it, then tossed leaves and branches on the grave and put the shovel in the wagon. Tiring work.

He leaned on the wagon and lighted a cigar. A good night's work, all right. Now he'd say that Penry had to make a fast trip East. Personal problems . . . that was good enough. Who would question him?

They might think it odd that Penry had left at night, but let them think it. He got back in the wagon and drove back to town.

• • •

Ki had slipped into town that night again, leaving his horse in the same place. He went down the alley past the privies and halted behind the Slipper, looking up at the window. Was it still open? He thought it was.

He peered around, making sure he was alone, then went close to the building. He was about to climb up when a window opened above him. Quickly he ducked behind a shed. He was astonished when he saw a body pushed from the window and lowered on a rope to the ground.

It was too dark to see who the deceased was.

In a few moments the back door of the saloon opened and Nails came out. Ki saw him clearly. Nails opened the near stable door, then carried the body inside.

In another moment Nails came out with a drawn revolver and peered around. But he went back inside, hitched up a light wagon, and drove away. Ki followed him at a distance, saw him turn off the road and stop. Ki dismounted and moved closer, close enough to see the grave and the body Nails rolled in. Who had Nails killed?

He had the answer next day. When young Joseph Canfield came to meet Sanchez, he told him the news. Nick Sanchez told Ramon. Vance Collworth had disappeared. He had not slept in his bed at the boardinghouse and not appeared at the Slipper.

Nails had told someone that Vance had taken the stage East because of a personal emergency.

Ki said, "The impostor is dead. Last night Nails buried him beside the road an hour out of town."

Carlos was startled. "Are you positive?"

"I saw the body. Last night I could not recognize him, but I marked the spot. We can dig him up."

"Then let's do," Ramon said.

Chapter 18

They decided to wait for nightfall. Digging up bodies, Ramon said, should always be done at night. It was the closest thing to a joke Jessica had ever heard Ramon utter. Perhaps he had read it somewhere.

She and Ki discussed the new development. What did it mean? Were the crooks beginning to fall out? Was Nails about to take flight? Or was he merely removing one division of the spoils?

Ki thought it was the latter. With a man like Nails, it must be like living with a powder keg. And "Vance" was never seen by anyone. Maybe his usefulness had gone, and Nails had eliminated him in his usual fashion.

With Ramon in the lead, Ki and Carlos went down the mountain, around the town, and along the road to the leaning rocks. It was a dark night with a misty overcast that smelled wet.

They had brought along a shovel and a bulldog lantern.

But when they arrived, the shovel was not needed. The grave was opened and the body was gone! Carlos played the yellow light on the hole as they all stared.

"He came and dug it up," Ki said.

"Why would he do that?"

"Because he's cagier than we thought." Ki kicked at the freshly turned earth. "He thought he heard me outside the stable, and now he's taking no chances."

"And he's buried the body somewhere else," Carlos said, sighing. "Now we'll never find it."

Nails did not know who had trailed him, but he was positive it was one of the Basques. He had driven the wagon back to the town, and out again in an hour, making certain this time that he was not followed.

This was done by halting the wagon and walking back along the road with a rifle, ready to fire at any shadow. But there was none.

He had dug up the body and hauled it another five miles and buried it mostly by caving in the banks of a dry gulch on it. The winter rains might lay it bare, but by then it would be only bones.

He knew the story of Collworth's going East in a hurry would be talked about—but who could prove different?

He sent for Tim Hickson and sat him down in the office. "Old Fernando Diaz is charged with the murder of Nate Smith. What're you doing about it?"

It was the first Hickson had heard of it.

Nails said, "Those Basques up on the mountain are protecting him. It's your job to bring him in here for justice."

"But that's a job for the county sheriff! I ain't got any jurisdiction there."

"Gimme your badge," Nails said, extending his hand.

"Wait a minute. I don't know about this here charge."

"Nate was gunned down by old Diaz. He's got to be brought in for a trial. What else you need t'know?"

"Well, is there witnesses, and any evidence that—"

"Gimme your goddamn badge. I see you're not the man for this job."

"Dammit, Nails! I'm tryin' to do the job!"

Nails pretended patience. "Go see Johnny Harris and Link. Link got shot in the leg. They both know what to say. Now get outta here." He pointed to the door.

Hickson hurried out. He knew Link, but not Harris. Link was a miner who had abandoned several claims and had done some odd jobs for Nails until he'd gotten shot. Hickson found him hobbling around the corral behind the saloon.

Yes, Link said, old Diaz had shot him, all right, the sonofabitch. "And he killed Nate with a knife. Quickest thing you ever seen."

"He shot you but he knifed Nate?" Hickson sat on the pole.

Link looked uncomfortable. "Yes, he did."

"Ain't that funny?"

"Maybe it is. I dunno. But that's what he did."

"All right." Hickson slid off the corral pole. "I got to talk to Harris. Where's he hang out?"

"He goin' tell you the exact thing I just did."

Hickson looked at him. "That the way you goin' tell it to the judge?"

"Damn right."

Hickson nodded. He was sure they both would. Or Nails would have their hides.

He went back to the office and sat behind the desk. How bad did he want to be town marshal? He was going to have Nails's foot on his neck every day, no doubt about it.

And now Nails was telling him to get men together and go up into the hills for old Diaz. No way he could go alone.

And it was probably suicide. A dozen men had already tried it, and four were dead. Those were terrible odds. The Basques knew that mountain like he knew his left thumbnail.

Hickson stared at the opposite wall. It was nice, being marshal, all the free drinks and free eats. But one day or one dark night, he might have to pay up—with his life. Just to keep Nails happy. Nails wasn't going up into the goddamn mountains!

He smoked a cigarette, staring into space. Then he got up and rode to his boardinghouse and packed the little he owned into a possibles bag and left it in a corner. He went down to supper, stopped in at the Alamo Saloon for a couple of beers, and when it got very dark he went back for the bag and rode quietly out of town. He never looked back.

A few miles from town he tossed the badge into the brush.

• • •

Jack English was a welcome addition to their little army. Ramon was delighted to have him. Including Ki and Carlos and himself, he had eleven men, and two of those were teen-aged boys. With Jack he had an even dozen.

"With me," Jessie said, "you have thirteen."

"That's unlucky."

"Only if you think so." Jessie attended Jack's wound again, changing the bandage. It was but a deep scratch, and he insisted he could hardly feel it.

"Your hands draw the pain away." He watched her put salve on the wound again and bind it up. "I am sorry it is such a trifle. You are such an excellent physician."

"And you a flatterer."

"Not at all. I speak only the truth."

She smiled at him. "How long will you stay with us?"

"I haven't straightened out my life yet. I mean, I don't know. I came here because I thought Nails would send men after me. He still may, you know."

He rose and put his coat on, easing the sleeve over the bandage. "Why don't you show me around."

"Of course."

They rode higher into the mountains, walking the horses, following trails barely seen. Now and again they halted to look back at the valley below, the town far in the distance with smoke staining the horizon.

The air was clear, with a fresh pine scent and a wandering breeze that rustled the tops of trees. In a little glade they got down and walked side by side along the mountain, leaving the horses to crop grass.

He asked, "Where are Mr. and Mrs. Diaz?"

"Carlos moved them back into the mountains. I'm not sure just where. I was there, but I doubt if I could find my way again unaided."

"You know that Nails has accused Mr. Diaz of murder?"

"Yes. A ridiculous charge."

They paused and Jack faced her. "Tell me something . . . why are you and Ki here? Do you have some reason for defending these people?"

"Only that they are our friends."

"That's a very good reason. But you came here without knowing them."

She smiled. "Yes. We came to find Vance Collworth."

"Collworth?" He was astonished. Then his face cleared. "Oh, yes . . . now I remember. You came into town asking about Collworth. But you never told me why."

"Because he and my father were old friends. But the Vance Collworth who runs the Slipper now is not the Vance Collworth I knew."

"He's changed?"

"He is not the same person. An impostor. Not the same man at all."

Jack sighed. "That would explain a lot of things." He glanced around, smiling. "I hope we can find the way back."

She turned, glancing down the slope and suddenly felt his hands slip over her shoulders. He kissed her cheek softly.

"You are a beautiful girl, Jessica."

"Thank you." She turned slightly, leaning back against him. "The way to get off a mountain is to go downhill."

He laughed. "How practical you are." He kissed her again.

She turned her lips to meet his. Then she took his hand and they went back to the horses.

★

Chapter 19

Nails sat in his office, thinking about the silver. A vein of it, a yard wide! But up there on the mountain.

Thank God he was the only one who knew of it.

But how to get possession? Undoubtedly the Basque's homestead deeds were good; he could depend on that. How could he push them off the mountain? If he went up there with men and slaughtered them, it would be impossible to keep it a secret—*if* he won the battle. He had lost the last time.

Maybe he could make it so uncomfortable for them that they would pull up stakes and leave.

But how many times had he heard how stubborn they were?

They had certain advantages, too. They knew the ground and he did not. And they had right on their side. Nails came close to a smile. Right. Had he ever worried about right? If he began worrying about *that,* he was through. Might makes right. It was his code, what he lived by.

But in this case, too much might would draw the law. The sheriff seldom came to Eagle Rock or sent a deputy. But he could happen by and ask difficult questions. . . .

So maybe a little might would do the trick. Harassment. The sheep killing had made them institute a guard system—which had worked against him in the long run. Nails scowled. The woman and her Chinaman friend were probably up there with the Basques. And he supposed Jack English had gone there as well.

What if he offered a bounty on them, any one of them? He could put out the offer in restricted circumstances, only among certain men—hard cases who would take risks for the right kind of money. Why not?

A determined man might slip into the mountains and find one or two of them alone. Nails actually smiled. He could whittle them down that way, all right.

It would cost money, but it would be worth it. And one day he would have the biggest silver mine in the country! He would dominate the market . . . buy out the small claims. Then he would *be* somebody! Not just the big fish in a small pond, but a big fish in a big pond!

But first things first. He must somehow root out the Basques because he saw them as standing in his way.

A determined man. Where would he find such a determined man? Probably not in Eagle Rock. The largest town within a reasonable distance was Stanton, in the next county. He would probably have to go there himself . . . he could not trust such a mission to an underling.

And then, as he was preparing to leave, the news was brought to him that Tim Hickson had disappeared.

Jed Miles, one of his saloon bouncers, brought him the word. "He ain't in the office, and he ain't at the boardinghouse."

"He had a horse."

"It's gone too."

"Did anyone see him go?"

Miles shook his head. "Ain't found anybody who did."

Nails waved the man out. He opened a box, took out a cigar, and bit off the end. Was it because he'd told Hickson to arrest old Diaz? Hickson knew that four men were dead because they'd raided into the mountains. Yes, that was probably it. Hickson hadn't had the balls for it.

He lit the cigar and puffed hard, feeling suddenly alone. Penry was gone, and now Hickson. Well, he'd always despised Penry, and Hickson was only a hired hand.

He got up and went down to the saloon. Several boys were sweeping out, as they did every morning, chairs up on the tables. His saloon manager was going over the accounts with one of the barmen, and he could hear hammering from the back. Every morning they had to repair a few chairs, sometimes a table.

When the manager, Slim Shepard, saw him he said something to the barman and came round the bar, brows lifted.

Nails said, "Everything all right?"

"Same as usual, Nails. Things're fine."

Nails took his arm and turned him; they walked toward the front door, which was locked. He said, "I'm going out of town for a few days, maybe three or four."

Shepard nodded. He asked no questions.

"How many bouncers do we have?"

Shepard glanced at him. "Three. There's usually two on duty at a time."

"Have any of them got any brains? I mean enough so they don't step in cow shit when they cross the street?"

The manager smiled. "Max can tie his shoes himself."

"All right. You tell Max he's town marshal, starting today. He can hire a deputy. I'll talk to him when I get back. Just keep the peace, is all."

Shepard was surprised. "What happened to Tim?"

"He quit."

Shepard made a face. "All right, Nails. I'll take care of it. You leaving today?"

"Yes." Nails went back upstairs.

It was Jessica who first asked, "What about the silver? Are you going to open a mine?"

Carlos said, "None of us are miners. How do you do those things?"

Carmelita agreed with Jessie. "Can't we pay someone to work them for us?"

"Where would we find them? The miners hereabouts are under Nails's thumb or scared to death of him."

"Go to Trinity," Carmelita said.

Jessie asked, "What's Trinity?"

"It's a town across the mountains. There's a stage, and a freighter there that connects with the railroad. If I remember, the tracks are some twenty miles away."

Carlos nodded. "Yes, we could do that. . . ."

Carmelita pointed her finger. "*You* could do that. Ramon is guarding us, so you go to Trinity. Isn't that fair?"

Carlos shrugged. Ki said, "I will go with him."

And so it was decided.

Ki had barely enough time to walk alone with Carmelita. She said, "You may be gone a week. . . . It is an eternity."

He smiled. "Some eternities pass very quickly. I will think of you every moment." He kissed her. "It should not be a difficult journey."

"I hope we are not being foolish to think of mining when we may be fighting for our lives."

"We can do both." He kissed her again. "But now I must pack, or Carlos will go without me."

Carmelita brought them food; they tied blanket rolls behind the saddle cantles, with a slicker each in case of rain, and set off up the mountain.

Carlos was sure of the way, though he said he had not been over that particular path for several years. He had brought along a machete in case the brush had overgrown the trail that led up a single-file switchback route to the ridge. They reached the ridge in several hours and rested the horses.

The view was spectacular, though a haze overlaid the country to the north and from their position they could not see the town.

They went east along the ridge, and, when it divided, went south.

At their elevation there was little underbrush and the path was clear for many miles and reasonably well marked. But when dusk approached they found a camping place under an overhang lest they lose the trail and themselves.

It was very quiet on the high mountain, hardly a breeze stirring. Far out over the valley a few birds soared, seeming to hang almost motionless, then disappearing in the haze. At the far horizon the retreating sun had left a residue of gold that slowly turned blood red in wavering streaks that gradually darkened until finally the light faded away.

Ki made a small fire in a crevice and they broiled meat and drank coffee. Then they rolled up and went to sleep.

In the morning they began the long descent, winding down toward the distant, misty prairie. Trinity was somewhere out there, Carlos said. It was mostly a cattle town, the largest town for many miles in any direction.

Jack English rode with Ramon, visiting each of the guard posts along the lower mountain, insisting that Ramon assign him a position. "I want to do my part."

"Very well." Ramon took him to the westernmost post. "You can start here." He explained the signals and what was expected of each man. Each stint was four hours long; Ramon would see him probably once an hour.

Jack left his horse in a nearby draw, took his rifle, and made himself comfortable in the trench that had been dug previously. The forest around him was silent except for a few small birds that chattered in friendly fashion far over his head. It was a warm day and he settled down to be watchful. He could see perhaps a hundred yards in front and to the sides; the ground sloped away steeply to his left. Nothing moved.

He set the Winchester on a little hillock of grass, pointing down the slope. In a half-hour he looked at his watch and was surprised that not more time had fled past. Putting the watch away he told himself not to look at it again until Ramon showed up.

Ramon took longer than an hour to make the rounds. This time he came on foot. Slipping through the trees like an Indian. He let Jack see him some distance away, then came in casually.

"Everything all right?"

"Nothing to report," Jack said cheerfully. "Is anybody going to come up here in the daytime?"

Ramon shrugged. "Can't tell. Your canteen full?"

"Full enough."

"Then see you later." Ramon waved and was gone.

No more than fifteen minutes had passed after Ramon had disappeared, when Jack heard the rasping voice behind him. "Lift your hands nice'n easy."

★

Chapter 20

Nails took the stage to Stanton, a two-day trip. He went alone and arrived late in the afternoon, tired and irritable, needing a bath.

Stanton was a trading center. A spur line of the railroad ended there, and the new section of the town was growing and prospering. The old section, where the saloons and dancehalls proliferated, got more sleazy and weatherbeaten every year. The old section of town was where Nails headed. That was where Bat Kroger lived.

Bat was an aging pistoleer. He had been everything, including a lawman, but he had ridden the owlhoot trail more often than anything else. There was more money in it by far and, unlike most of his ilk, he'd had the sense to put something by for the days when he wouldn't be up to rolling in a blanket on the hard ground with a posse beating the brakes looking for him.

He lived quietly in the Muller Hotel and spent his evenings sipping beer in one of the nearby saloons, telling lies with his cronies and keeping abreast of the gossip.

Nails had known Bat in Texas where both had gone one winter for health reasons. If anyone would be able to tell him what he wanted to know, Nails thought it would be Bat.

He went directly from the stagecoach terminal to the Muller Hotel and signed for a room. "Is Mr. Kroger still living here?"

"Yes, sir."

"Where'll I find him?"

"I don't rightly know, sir." The clerk was a kid, still wet behind the ears. "He ain't in his room."

"You saw him go out?"

The lad nodded. "An hour ago, about."

Nails went up to his room, then back downstairs to the bathhouse adjoining the hotel, where he soaked in a tub for a half-hour. Bat had still not returned when he got out, so Nails laid on the bed for a nap and woke later to a rapping on the door.

It was Bat. "Kid said you was looking for me. Howdy, Nails. Long time. What the hell you doin' here?"

"Business," Nails said. "Come on in." Bat looked older, very gray, but he was still a big man with round shoulders and a paunch. He was wearing an old brown coat and wrinkled pants; he looked like a rancher come to town for a look at the shows. He tossed his hat onto a table and flopped in a chair by a window.

Nails sat opposite. He and Bat had never been close, more acquaintances than anything else, being in the same trade at the same time. He said, "You retired, Bat? Taking it easy?"

"Only a damn fool goes huntin' trouble when he don't have to. I ain't been outside of town here f'five year."

Nails smiled. "You're not wanted anywhere?"

Bat shook his head. A sly smile crept over his leathery face. "They don't know 'bout ever'thing a man ever done, and of course I can't remember. . . ."

"You playing it smart, Bat." Nails nodded solemnly. "Don't know anybody else kept more'n a dollar of that easy money."

"It fritters," Bat agreed. He pulled at a corner of his gray mustache. "What you want t'see me about?"

"I need a hard case. Somebody without too much worry and lots of guts. Also somebody not too goddamn expensive."

Bat looked out the window and worried his chin. "This feller, he going to work alone?"

"Probably. Not nailed down, though."

"I see." Bat thought about it, eyes narrowed and fingers moving on the grizzled chin. "You lookin' for brains too?"

Nails shrugged. "Enough to come in outta the rain. The job won't call for no particular brainwork."

Bat brought his gaze in from the window. He looked at the brass bedstead, at the carpet, at the brown pictures on the wall. "This feller have to go up against very many?"

"You mean at a time?" Nails shook his head. "It depends on how dumb he is."

"I c'n give you a name. You care if he's a kid?"

"No."

"He about twenty, I figger. Name of Earl Miller. Prob'ly not his real name. But you don't care 'bout that. They call him Early. I think he'll do you."

"Where'll I see this kid?"

"I'll send somebody for him. He ain't in town. Prob'ly take a few days. You got the time?"

"I'll have to make it. You figure he's the best for the job?"

Bat shrugged lightly and smiled. "Kid like him, he figgers to live forever. Guts by the bucket. I wouldn' run him for governor, but he c'n get on and off a horse by hisself."

"What'll he cost me?"

Bat shook his head. "You got to make your own deal. But if there's killin' in it, I don't want to hear no more. We never had this here conversation."

Nails nodded. "That's right. We didn't."

It was three days before Early Miller rode into town, put up his horse at the livery, and looked up Nails. Nails took him upstairs to the room and locked the door behind them. The kid looked slightly older than twenty, smooth-faced, and catlike in his movements. He had colorless eyes and wore a shoulder holster under his coat.

"You married?" Nails asked.

"No."

"Ever been in Eagle Rock?"

Early shook his head.

"That's good. Bat tell you anything about—?"

"Nothing. I come because Bat asked me."

"You know how t'use that gun?"

The kid made a movement and the pistol was in his hand, thumb on the hammer.

Nails nodded approvingly. He spent twenty minutes going over the situation at Eagle Rock and the mountain, not making light of the problem as he saw it. Early listened intently, no expression on his smooth face. His brows raised slightly when he heard that a strange woman and a Chinaman were involved, but in answer to Nails's question he said he had not heard of them.

When Nails finished, Early asked, "What you want me t'do?"

"You're on the payroll the day you leave for Eagle Rock, and I give you a bonus for each of them Basques or the others that you get rid of—permanent."

The kid nodded slowly. "I do it my way?"

"Any goddamn way you want, just so's it gets done. But don't come walking in the Slipper for payment. We'll have to meet somewheres."

The kid nodded again. Nails had a crude map of the entire area and they studied it together. He would not go into Eagle Rock at all, Early said, but slide into the mountain from the east and feel his way. He would give them no warning.

Nails was very pleased. He gave the kid a payment in gold in advance, and the next morning, alone, took the stage back to Eagle Rock, feeling that at last something definite was going to happen.

He was surprised, when he arrived, to learn that Jack English was in the local jail.

He was told that Jed Miles and two others had been scouting the lower mountain reaches and had come across Ramon Diaz's line of outposts.

They had been looking for them, expecting to find some such, Jed told him. And he had snuck up on the last one of the line and found it to be occupied by Jack English.

"Why'd you bring him back?" Nails asked.

Jed shrugged. "A shot would'a brought some others, maybe."

"Yes, maybe," Nails growled. He waved the man out.

★

Chapter 21

At midday Ki and Carlos paused in the foothills, high enough to overlook the flats, and watched the dust devils whirl far below them. Ki thought he could see the roofs of the town in the distance, but maybe it was some trick of the prairie. Carlos said the town was at least twenty miles away.

They did not reach the town till dusk.

Trinity straddled the old trade path east and west, and possibly owed its existence to the fact that it also hugged a spring-fed lake. A few houses had sprung up on the edges of the lake. Someone had built a store there, and in a decade there were five or six hundred people eking out a living, trading or farming or running a few cattle in the neighborhood.

There was even a hotel in a town that now boasted at least a thousand souls. And a dozen women, not counting dance-hall girls.

They put up at the hotel and let it be known they were looking for miners. There was a saloon attached to the hotel and they made certain everyone in it knew of their search. They did the same in each of the saloons.

The second day their search bore fruit. They were sitting in tilted-back chairs on the walk in front of the hotel when a rough-looking man approached and said his name was Murphy and that he was a miner. He certainly looked like a miner.

"What kinda ore you after, gents?"

"Silver," Carlos said. "We've got a claim in the mountains, over by Eagle Rock."

"I been there," Murphy said, shaking his head. "You work for Nails?"

"I'm afraid Nails is an enemy of ours."

Murphy smiled. "In that case, tell me about your mine."

On his next round, Ramon discovered that Jack English was not in position. From the tracks, he deduced that several men had taken Jack away. He was not a tracker, but it was no trick to follow the trail down the slopes to the road that led to Eagle Rock.

Jack must have dozed off and they had closed in. He was probably now in the town jail.

When he returned to the house and told them, the others were shaken by the news. Carmelita feared Nails would put Jack in front of a kangaroo court and have him executed.

She said, "We should find out what he intends."

"That means someone has to go into town."

Ramon said, "I'll go visit the Canfields. They can tell us the local news and gossip."

No one had a better idea.

Joseph Canfield was due with his light wagon, and when he arrived late at night and the wagon unloaded, Ramon went back with him. The lad's parents were still up waiting for him, and they were surprised to see Ramon.

Elmer Canfield was running to fat about the middle: a dumpy man, but even-tempered and patient. His wife, Maria, was small and wiry, and the lad, Joseph, was like neither of them—and yet like both. He put the horse and wagon away in the stable as Ramon hurried into the house.

"What're you doing here?" Elmer asked. "If they catch you God knows what they'll do to you!"

Maria put the coffeepot on the stove and they sat about the kitchen table as Ramon told them about the raid and about Jack English being taken.

"I haven't heard nothing about Jack," Elmer said. "He's maybe in the jail, then. But Nails ain't in town."

"Where's he gone?"

Elmer shrugged. "Don't know. Talk is, nobody's seen him for two, three days."

Maria poured the coffee. "What about your father?"

"He's fine. Can you get me a sketch of the jail?"

Elmer made a face. "I never been in that office. The jail's right behind the office, you know."

"I been in it," Joseph spoke up. They all looked at him and he said quickly, "Marshal paid me a dime to sweep it out one day."

"Well," Ramon said, "get the boy a piece of paper and a pencil. Can you remember the layout, Joe?"

"Sure, I think so."

His mother provided the back of an old letter and a sharpened pencil. Joseph bit his lip and stared at the paper for a moment, then drew a careful rectangle.

"Is this a floor plan?" Ramon asked.

The lad nodded. "This part is the jail. There's four cells, two on each side of the center aisle. I think some of the cells have windows . . . they're high up, with bars."

The boy frowned. "I don't know. But I think it's flat." He went back to the drawing. "This's the front door off the street, and this's the door to the jail. They keep the keys to the cells on a big ring that hangs here, by the door."

Ramon studied the drawing. "Maybe the easiest way in is by the front door." He looked at the boy. "Anything else?"

"Well, there's always somebody in the office." He glanced at his father. "Are you fixin' to break out Mr. English?"

"We're thinking about it," Ramon said. "Do two people ever stay all night?"

The boy didn't know. "But there's a cot in the office."

"I'll find a reason to go by there tomorrow," Elmer promised. "Maybe I can spot something."

Ramon shook his head. "Maybe you better not. Somebody might remember—after we go in after Jack. We don't want to attract attention to you."

"That's right, dear," Maria said. "Let the young ones do this."

Elmer nodded reluctantly.

Ramon rode back to the foothills with Joseph up behind on the horse. When he got down, the boy rode the horse back and put him in the stable.

Ramon put the drawing in front of them, sitting around a table. "Can we wait for Ki and Carlos to get back?"

Carmelita looked at her brother. "You rush into everything. I wonder you weren't married years ago."

He was astonished. "What has marriage got to do with breaking a man out of jail?"

She ignored that. "We have to wait for them. What do you think, Jessie?"

"I agree. But Ramon is right that time could be critical. If Nails—"

"Nails is out of town, according to the Canfields. So maybe there is time. I'll slip into the town tonight and look at the jail again. What if they've taken him somewhere else?"

"That's bad," Jessica said, frowning. "But where else would they take him?"

Ramon shook his head.

He went down the mountain that night shortly after dark. He left the horse in a ravine outside of town and moved by back ways to a point near the jail, where he could watch it. If Jack English was inside, wouldn't someone take him food? It was the middle of the week so it was unlikely there would be anyone else in the cells. The marshal usually locked up drunks over the weekends.

The jail was seldom used for anything but drunks.

His guess proved right. In less than an hour a boy came from one of the restaurants with a covered tray, delivering it to the jail.

He could be pretty sure that that was where Jack was.

• • •

Nails debated a charge against Jack English. He could hardly charge the man with murder when two men had tried to kill him in front of a dozen witnesses.

Jack had only fired in self-defense.

And it was hardly a crime for Jack to call Nails names . . . and dare him to do anything about it. Nails was smart enough to know that everyone in town would side against him.

But not very many knew that Jack was in the jail.

He ought to be able to do something about that. Maybe Early Miller could help. That made him smile. No one could know the thread of connection between them.

But in order to do that, he'd have to find Miller and meet with him. Early Miller was a lone wolf and now that he'd been given a trail to follow he would not be easy to locate. He would probably have to wait until Miller found him.

Maybe that wouldn't be long. And in the meantime Jack could rest in jail. It would do him good.

★

Chapter 22

Ki and Carlos spent considerable time with Sean Murphy, the miner. They also interviewed four other men, but came back to Murphy each time. There was an assay office in Trinity and they listened to the assay proprietor and Murphy discuss mining and ores and decided Murphy was their man.

He was only thirty, but had prospected the entire vast area with unfortunately little success. The Eagle Rock area had attracted him, he said, but there had been unexplained killings and mine takeovers, and the attraction had faded. If a man made a strike he was liable to wake up in the morning—dead, Murphy said. No one could prove anything, but fingers were pointed at Nails.

Murphy was slim, a little bedraggled, clothes torn, hair too long; it had been a while since he'd made any kind of strike, he told them. He'd been doing odd jobs, trying to get a grubstake together. With some tools, a mule and food, he would set out again toward the north—but he eagerly accepted their proposition. He would work their mine for a share. They shook on it.

They bought him clothes and tools, and a haircut. Ki

bought a thick-legged black mule and a wooden tree, a roan horse and second-hand saddle. They spent an hour in the general store, packed the goods on the mule, and were off before midday, riding toward the mountains.

Murphy proved to be a good companion. He was cheerful but not garrulous, and by the end of the first day it was as if he had been with them for months.

He was a willing worker when they made camp, and was a better cook than either of them, for which they were grateful.

He was not, however, any good with weapons, he confessed. All his fights had been with fists; he had never owned a gun of any kind, and was a little wary of them. Their first day in the mountains, Carlos, at a rest stop, tried to show Murphy how to shoot a rifle. He put up a target at a dozen yards and showed the miner how to aim. But Murphy was inclined to close his eyes and yank the trigger, and never succeeded in coming anywhere close to the target. Carlos gave up.

"I know the blasted thing is goin' to kick my shoulder," Murphy said plaintively.

"But if you squeeze the trigger the shot will be away before the kick," Carlos explained.

"But it still kicks," Murphy said.

They tried him with a revolver. But he still yanked the trigger, sending the shot wide each time. And his grip on the pistol was so tight that Carlos regretted ever teaching him.

"Leave me be," Murphy said with a grin. He doubled up his big fist. "If one of them claim-jumpers gets close enough, I'll fix his buttons."

Ramon was sitting on the porch of the house in the settlement, smoking a cigar with a rifle across his knees when they arrived.

He looked Murphy over carefully when they introduced him. Murphy took off his hat courteously and they shook hands. Ramon explained that Carmelita and Jessica had gone to the cabin to take supplies to his father and mother and would be back before nightfall.

"There's still light," Murphy said. "Is the mine close by?"

"I'll take you there," Ki offered, climbing back on his horse.

Murphy followed him, leading the mule. The two prospectors' holes were under a cliff face. The dirt had been filled in, but Murphy quickly shoveled out the loose earth and got down to the ore . . . and sat down, looking, smelling and handling it.

"What's the matter?" Ki asked. "Isn't it silver?"

"Oh, it's silver all right." Murphy smiled up at him. "But silver is usually found with copper, lead and zinc, and sometimes with gold. You've got all of them here or my name is O'Hooligan."

"Is there enough to mine?"

Murphy laughed. "Good enough, he says! I've never seen such rich ore!" He climbed out of the hole. "There's no telling how far the vein goes, but we'll find that out when we start diggin' seriously." He pulled out the makin's and began to roll a cigarette. "The next question is, where's the smelter?"

Ki shrugged elaborately. "I suppose there's one in Eagle Rock . . . but I don't know."

Murphy put the cigarette in his mouth and struck a match. "Well, we can take out this here ore and put it in sacks, but it's got to be hauled somewheres." He grinned. "I'll get it out'n the ground. You get it to the smelter."

They discussed the problem that night, sitting around the table in the main room of the house. Carmelita and Jessica had returned and were delighted to see Murphy, who bowed to them in courtly fashion.

The ore was safe in the ground, Murphy told them after hearing the situation in Eagle Rock. "Or we can dig it up and put it in sacks—you'll have to provide hundreds of sacks—and we can stack it, ready for hauling."

Carlos asked, "Why can't we haul it to Trinity on muleback? From there it can go to a smelter."

Murphy nodded. "That's so, but you'll attract prospectors by the dozen. There's no more curious set of folks on earth than miners. They'll be all over this mountain pokin' and diggin'."

Ki said, "So Eagle Rock is the best bet."

"If we get rid of Nails first," Ramon added.

"There's one other thing," Ki said. He indicated Murphy.

"We promised Murphy a share, and his share is worth nothing if the ore's still in the ground."

"Oh, it's worth a good deal," Murphy said quickly. "I can wait. I've waited for years for a strike like this one. Don't you worry about me." He looked round the table at them. "In the meantime I can explore a bit, see where the vein goes. . . ."

"All right," Carlos said, "is that the decision? We leave it in the ground till we can take it into Eagle Rock?" He smiled as they nodded. "Let's hope that's not too far off."

"What about Jack English?" Ramon asked.

"That's the next question." Carlos spread the floor plan of the jail on the table. "Ramon says maybe the best way in is through the front door but it's thick and it's also locked at night. Any suggestions?"

"If you want to go in the front door," Murphy said, "why not blast it open?"

"Blast it with what?"

"Dynamite," Murphy said in surprise.

Ramon looked at him. "We don't know anything about dynamite."

Murphy shrugged. "I been using it for years. You get me a couple sticks and I'll take that door off sweet as you please."

Carmelita laughed. She jumped up and ran around the table to kiss his cheek. "This man is a treasure!"

Carlos asked, "Can we get dynamite from the Canfields?"

"We can ask. I'm sure Elmer will find us some."

"I'll go there tonight," Carlos said.

It was a dark night, with only a wisp of moon, when Ki met Carmelita at the edge of the woods. They walked hand in hand along the ghost of a trail, far above the houses where lights twinkled like fireflies.

Ki had brought a blanket, and he spread it on the grass in a circle of pines and they lay down, gazing at the dark sky.

"It's like a Druids' circle," he said softly.

"What's that?"

"It's what some call a circle of pines. The ancient pine in the center drops seeds in a circle, and when the old pine dies the young ones grow up in a ring around the place."

"That must take a long time."

"A century or more, I suppose. Nature takes its time about a lot of things. It's man who's in a hurry."

She moved closer, slipping an arm across his chest, kissing his cheek. "We are not trees."

He embraced her tenderly. "I had noticed that." He kissed her and for a long time they did not speak. It was an hour before he rolled away and they sat up. The tiny arc of moon had gone and it seemed darker . . . and more silent under the trees. Hardly a whisper of wind brushed the pinetops.

Ki rolled up the blanket and they walked back toward the settlement slowly—until he halted her suddenly, pressing a finger to her lips. His eyes searched the shadows below them. Had he seen a horseman walking there? It could not be Ramon or one of his men; they were far below, near the foot of the mountains.

Carmelita put her lips to his ear. "What is it?"

"I thought I saw a horseman." He took her arm and they moved carefully down the slope till Ki halted. "It was right about here . . ."

She whispered, "What would a horseman be doing here?"

He shrugged. "Maybe looking over the land—testing our guard for a later raid." He knelt and felt for tracks, but the ground was harder here. *Had* he seen the man?

They waited for a time, but the mysterious horseman did not reappear.

When he told Ramon, the Basque was very concerned. "We don't have the men to watch everywhere." He waved his arm. "There could be forty men in the timber and we wouldn't know it."

"Until they killed us."

"Yes. We would know it then."

Chapter 23

Carlos went to see the Canfields late at night and brought back several sticks of dynamite. Elmer Canfield kept it in stock. One stick would be enough, Murphy said, to take off the door of the jail and part of the wall with it.

Ramon was disinclined to wait. "We've got the dynamite . . . let's do it right away!"

Carlos was more cautious. "We don't know what we're up against."

"Does Nails know we're going to dynamite the door? How could he guess that?"

"We ought to make sure we're not walking into a buzz saw."

Jessica said, "You're both right. But maybe we ought to take the chance. We want Jack out of that jail."

"You hear that?" Ramon demanded. "Nails is capable of anything. Murphy and I will do it tonight!"

"Then I'll go along," Carlos said.

"Let me go instead," Ki insisted. "I know something about explosives."

"Wait a minute." Jessie rapped on the table with her

knuckles. "Sean has to go because he's our dynamite expert. But he doesn't need anyone else, except for company. So I will go with him."

"You're guessing at who's inside the jail," Carlos replied. "When the blast knocks the door down we still have to get the key and go in for Jack. Murphy is no hand with a gun—I've seen him shoot. He couldn't hit the barn from ten feet. There has to be three of us."

They drew straws finally, and Carlos and Jessica won.

It was a good night for it. The weather was turning, summer was past and fall was before them with ground fog clouding the paths as they rode down the mountain long after dark.

Carlos led the way, walking his horse as they approached the town. They halted with the buildings in the distance, the lights haloed by mist, the street very quiet.

But when they moved closer they saw that the jail office was well lighted. The two small windows had some kind of cloth over them on the inside which showed the illumination but made it impossible for anyone to see into the room. The heavy door was closed though light seeped around one edge and the bottom.

"Could be a dozen men in there," Carlos said musingly.

"Maybe Nails figured we'd try to break Jack out."

Carlos nodded. He looked at the dark sky, then back at the jail. He smiled slightly at them. "Do we go in there unannounced?"

"Not smart," Ki said.

Murphy cleared his throat. "I can blow the front of the building off. . . ."

"If there's a troop of cavalry inside we'd be giving away our plan of attack for nothing." Ki shook his head. "I'm for waiting."

Murphy said, "We could blow the back of the building off."

Ki said, "The building is made of cement and fieldstones. You might kill everybody in the jail end."

Murphy sighed. "There's that . . ."

Carlos reluctantly agreed that they should wait. As they rode back into the mountains, Ki said, "Ramon told us that a boy delivered food to the jail. Tomorrow we'll stop the boy on his way out and ask him who's inside."

Carlos laughed. "I should have thought of that!"

The next day a light rain came whirling over the mountains, pattering down, accompanied by a thin mist that overlaid the valley. The rain came and went, drizzling and stopping fitfully.

When they rode down the mountain at night, the rain had gone but the mist remained. In a few months winter would be upon them. They left the horses near the end of town with Murphy to hold them, and Ki and Carlos took up station near the jail to watch for the boy.

They waited an hour before he appeared, rapped on the jail door and was admitted. He remained inside for less than a half-hour and when he reappeared, Carlos and Ki confronted him.

The lad was about fourteen, wiry and towheaded. His eyes went round when he recognized Carlos as a Basque. "We're not going to hurt you," Carlos said in friendly fashion.

"What you want, then?"

"Who's in the office?"

The boy seemed to relax. He even tried a faint smile. "You after Mr. English?"

"He's a friend of ours," Ki admitted.

"The office . . ." Carlos urged.

"They's three. Max Cotton is marshal now. He got two others with him. I don't know their names. There's one other man in the jail too."

Ki asked, "Is Max well liked in the town?"

The boy shook his head and his expression changed. "'Course not."

Carlos looked over the boy's head to the jail. "Are they expecting us?"

"Well—they talk about it."

Carlos said gently, "All right. You've got a chance to raise a fuss about us—or you can keep quiet. We won't say a word. No one will know you talked to us."

The lad nodded. "Ever'body knows Max and the others work for Nails. I won't say nothing."

"Good boy," Carlos said. He and Ki shook hands solemnly with the lad.

He asked, "You going in there now?"

Carlos indicated the street. "You best get along there—you can watch, but get behind something."

The lad nodded again, his eyes round. He hurried up the street.

While Ki watched the jail, Carlos went back for Murphy and his explosives.

The Irishman asked, "Shall I use both sticks?"

"Will one do the trick?"

Murphy grinned. "The door'll be matchsticks."

"Then use one," Carlos told him and Murphy went across the dark street to the jail.

They retreated to a corner of a building and watched. Murphy paused by the jail door, then a match flared and Murphy hurried back across the street. He was grinning, holding up five fingers.

Murphy had barely reached the building's corner when the explosion came. It shattered the night with a tremendous *boom!* The wooden door dissolved in a shower of splinters and a large, ragged hole appeared where the door had been. Someone inside screamed.

"Come on!" Carlos said urgently. He ran to the jail, his revolver out, Ki at his heels.

The office was a white haze of dust. Two lanterns had been burning, but both were smashed on the floor. Somehow a single candle had survived the blast and by its mealy light they saw that two men were unconscious on the floor. Another was yelling in pain, holding his leg.

Carlos pushed Murphy. "Get their guns."

Ki grabbed the ring with the jail keys and ran through the door to the back, spitting out dust.

Jack English, in an end cell, was holding the bars, staring at him. "Ki!"

Ki began trying keys in the lock. "Get your things together, Jack."

"I got nothing. What happened? Did you blow the goddamn door?"

"Dynamite," Ki replied. He found the right key and the

door squeaked open. Jack rushed out. There was another prisoner, yelling at them to let him out, but they ignored him.

Carlos was standing in the ragged door hole, watching the street. Murphy was outside, three gunbelts over his shoulder. They ran for the horses.

Jack rode behind Murphy and they headed for the foothills. "First jailbreak I ever tried," Carlos said, grinning.

"Nothing to it," Ki said.

★

Chapter 24

Esteban was dead when Ramon made his rounds. The man was slumped over the short trench, dead from a heavy blow on the head. The body was still warm; it had happened shortly before he arrived, Ramon thought.

It was a dark night, darker under the pines. He sat by the body, pistol in hand, searching the slope with his eyes. Could the murderer be far off?

He recalled the mysterious horseman Ki had seen. Was a murderer loose among them? He felt miserable; how could he face Esteban's family! He cocked and recocked the pistol in anger. If only the man would show himself—just for a moment! Had Nails sent someone to kill them off, one by one?

There were others along the hill. He would have to change the guard at once, leave two men together instead of one. That way they'd have a better chance against an intruder in the dark.

He pulled the body from the trench and laid it out so that it would not be doubled up when rigor came. Then he saw to the guards.

The death of Esteban was a blow to them all. What did it bode for the future?

"It proves," Carlos said, "that someone can roam the mountain without our discovering him."

"But we'll be more watchful now," Ki added.

"He has to sleep somewhere," Ramon said, "probably during the day. Where's the best place for that?"

"The caves," Carlos said at once, and Ramon nodded.

"What's that?"

Carlos explained. "Once, a long time ago, there was a river a few miles from here. It's dried up now—we think it went underground. Anyway, along one bank is a series of caves. Ramon and I used to play there as kids. This killer could hide there during the day."

"But there are a lot of caves," Ramon said. "The river made some long curves and along one side are caves, miles of them."

"Horses leave tracks," Carmelita said.

"We're counting on that," Ramon agreed.

Ramon, Ki, Jessica, and Carlos rode toward the caves the next morning. When they reached the wide, dry wash where the river had been, they spread out and walked the horses, looking for tracks.

There was no easy way to do it. The caves were off to the right, mostly little but overhanging cliff that had been gouged out by water action, probably for centuries. But occasionally, as Carlos explained, the caves went deep into the cliff where a camp fire could not be seen from outside. In some of the caves there was room for a dozen horses.

They saw no tracks.

"A clever man could have covered them," Ki said. "He would know that you would think of the caves."

"In that case," Jessie offered, "he might leave a few tracks here, to keep our attention—and go somewhere else."

"The nights are getting colder," Carlos said. "A cave would be better than sleeping under the trees somewhere."

Carmelita sighed when they returned to the house. "It means he could be anywhere. We must keep the windows covered at night."

"What about your father and mother?" Ki asked. "Would it not be safer to bring them back here?"

Carmelita bit her lip, and Carlos exchanged glances with his brother. It was obviously a hard question.

"They are far away from here," Carlos said hesitantly. "This murderer, whoever he is, will not know of them. How could he?"

"Still, it might be safer," Carmelita said. "*I* would feel better." She looked at Ramon, who nodded.

"I will go for them when it gets dark."

Nails walked down to look at the ruined jail. Max Cotton was at home in bed, bruised from head to toe. One of his deputies was in much the same condition; the other had two broken legs from flying rocks, but was otherwise coherent. He had been sitting behind a filing cabinet, which had absorbed the blast.

The office was destroyed but the jail was intact. The lone prisoner related how a man had come running in and had freed Jack English and taken him along with him.

Nails was disgusted. The blast had taken place late at night, and probably the men in the office were dozing. They were lucky all three hadn't been killed.

He ordered the cell opened and told the prisoner to get out. Then he sent for men to repair the office.

But no one wanted to be town marshal.

Nails went back to his own office and thought about it. He would probably have to import one from outside. What he needed was another man like Early Miller. And he was not likely to get him. Men who were really handy with a six-gun were few and far between. And too many who were handy were loners who wouldn't take the job for any consideration.

Well, the town could get along without a marshal for a while. He had his own bouncers in the Slipper. . . .

So he was not prepared for a visit from the county sheriff, John Collins.

Collins came riding in unannounced, with a young deputy at his heels, and stopped first at the jail, which was being reconstructed. The workers told him there was no one inside in the cells and suggested he talk to Nails.

Collins asked, "What happened here?"

"Dynamite," a mason told him. "Somebody blew the front offen the building."

"What for?"

"To bust somebody out."

"Anyone killed?"

"No. Hurt bad, though."

Collins went on to the Slipper and asked to see Nails. A bartender looked at the star on his shirt and hurried. Nails came downstairs immediately and offered to buy the sheriff a drink. "This is an honor, Sheriff."

"No thanks, I seldom drink anymore. Where can we talk, Nails?"

"Come upstairs." He led the way to his office and closed the door firmly.

Collins said, in his slow and deliberate way, "I hear odd things about this town, Nails. You told me a year ago that you'd see to the local law. Now I hear you can't find a man for the job."

"Who told you that?"

Collins waved a hand. "I hear things. Is it true?"

Nails sighed. "The local marshal was hurt in the blast and won't be on his feet for a bit. I've sent for another man." That wasn't exactly true, but Collins couldn't be expected to know it.

"Who broke who out of jail?"

"Gents unknown broke Jack English out. I think it was them goddamn Basques up on the mountain."

"Jack English? He was a deputy here."

Nails nodded. "For a while. Then he killed a couple men and took off for the mountains. Couple of my men brought him back."

Collins rolled a brown cigarette slowly. "Why don't you get along with the Basques?"

"Hell, they're foreigners, Sheriff. They got those funny foreign ways and they don't give a damn for the law—"

"I've never had complaints before."

"Well, they do things their way—and it ain't our way. They just don't fit in."

Collins lit the cigarette and puffed for a moment. "I've

talked to the Basques, you know. Seemed like nice folks. They don't exactly agree with what you say." He leaned forward. "Are you hasslin' them?"

"Of course not! Hell, I got my own troubles here. Them goddamn miners raise all the hell—what I want to go up on that goddamn mountain for?"

"I was just askin'," Collins said mildly. "So you got no claim on their land?"

"Absolutely not! I d'want any piece of it. Did they say I did?"

"No . . ."

Nails pounded the table beside him. "But they come down here and bust up our jail! They the ones who start trouble, Sheriff. No matter what they tell you."

"Umm. Why did Jack English take up with them? He was a deputy here."

"I got no idea . . . except one."

"What's that?"

"One of them Basque girls is awful pretty. And Jack, he allus had an eye for women."

"Izzat so." Collins reached and stubbed out the cigarette. He regarded Nails quizzically for a moment. "They tell me that Vance Collworth left here all of a sudden to go East. Is that a fact?"

"As far as I know."

"You were partners, weren't you?"

"Yes."

"Why didn't he tell you?"

Nails made a face. "It surprised me as much as anybody. Vance didn't tell me much—he didn't tell anybody much. A damn close-mouthed man. He said he was going and had a right to go— Hell, I didn't try to stop him."

"Why did he go?"

"He said he got a wire, but he didn't show it to me."

"Hmm. Is he coming back?"

"The last thing he said to me was he wouldn't be long, a month maybe. I got a hunch it was some family thing."

"Where did he come from?"

"I dunno. I met him in Kansas City. He kept our books,

you know. He was very good at that." Nails's voice had turned silky.

"Uh huh. Have you got another one—bookkeeper, I mean?"

"No. Vance'll be back. He'll come in one day on the stage, and it'll be like he never left."

"All right." Collins pushed his beefy frame out of the chair and stood for a moment looking down at Nails. "I brought along a young deputy. I'm going to leave him here in town for a bit to see you got no troubles. His name is Jim Zucker. He'll report to me ever' day by wire." Collins smiled. "I don't want you to have no troubles with the Basques."

"That's good of you, Sheriff."

Collins nodded with a smile. "Maybe you'll remember that at election time." He went out and closed the door behind him.

Nails sank back, his jaw gritting in anger. That sonofa-bitching meddling sheriff!

Chapter 25

As he had promised, Ramon went in the morning to bring his parents back to the main house. Carlos took his place making the rounds of the foothill watchers. They were fewer in number than at night, and they were placed much closer to the town.

Ramon's errand was uneventful. He helped with the packing and brought them both back to the house, seeing no one. When they arrived he took his father aside and explained the situation as it had developed. A killer was loose among them and until he was caught or eliminated, they must take every precaution.

Fernando agreed, though it galled him to stay inside.

While Ramon brought his parents back, Ki and Jessie rode to the upper meadows to check on the sheep. They had scattered, with no dogs or herders to keep them in flocks, but there were no bodies. The killer had confined himself to men, apparently.

That night, close to morning, young Pedro Deppe was found dead at his station. On hearing the signal, Ramon hurried to the spot. Pedro had been knifed in the back. The knife was missing.

The killing had taken place during a five- or ten-minute period when his partner, Manuel, had gone down the slope to answer a call of nature. To his consternation he had found the body on his return, and had instantly signaled Ramon.

The tooled belt young Deppe had been wearing was also missing. Manuel insisted that Pedro had been wearing it and that the killer must have taken it.

Later that morning in the main house Ramon faced the rest of them. "It means that the killer was close enough to watch them, waiting for his chance."

"He's got nerve . . ."

Ki had examined the body. "I think the knife was thrown from a distance. Then he went in to retrieve it and take the belt."

"Good knife throwers are not common," Carlos said. "Could he be that accurate?"

Ki pointed to the opposite wall. "Do you see that drop of paint just beside the window?" They turned their heads and in that instant heard a *thunk*. A knife was quivering in the center of the paint splotch, the point two inches into the wood.

Carmelita laughed and the others, except for Jessica, were astonished.

"You make your point," Carlos said, smiling.

Ki went across the room and retrieved the knife. "Why did the killer take the belt?"

"He liked it," Ramon suggested.

Ki shook his head. "Did the killer take anything from the body of Esteban?"

"Is it important?" Carmelita asked.

"It could be."

"Then I will find out." She went to the door.

Ki said, "If this killer has been sent to kill us one by one, how is his employer going to know he has done as he says?"

"By taking something from each victim!" Ramon exclaimed. "Of course!" He snapped his fingers. "Pedro's name was on the belt. I have seen it many times."

Carmelita was gone half an hour. When she returned she

said, "The killer took a small knife from Esteban's pocket. They did not find it with his effects."

Jessie asked, "Was his name on it?"

"Yes. You think the killer took it because of that?"

"It's a kind of tally," Carlos said. "Now he has killed two of us."

"And we don't know who he is or what he looks like." Ramon paced the room. "I think I should take the men from the watching posts. We can form roving patrols instead."

"It's worth a try," Ki agreed.

"I think we should try to find out where this killer sleeps. It must be here in the mountains. He probably sleeps in the daytime . . . maybe closer than the caves."

"He has a horse," Ki said, "if it was him I saw that night. A horse is a difficult animal to hide."

"Why not divide the area into sectors?" Jessie suggested.

"We haven't enough men to do it properly," Carlos said. "I think Ramon is right about the roving patrols."

"Then I'd better get to it." Ramon went out quickly.

Sheriff Collins learned that Ned Hilton had not been marshal for some time. When he asked about it, he was told that Ned had gotten himself drunk one night and had disappeared.

"What do you mean, disappeared?" Collins stood in the Alamo Saloon, frowning at the men around him.

"He just up and disappeared, Sheriff. One day he was here, next day he was gone. Ain't showed up since."

"Who paid him?"

"Merchants' Association."

Collins nodded. "That mean Nails?"

The men around him agreed it probably did. One offered, "Tim Hickson, he was made marshal."

"Is he still here?"

"No, he rode out too."

"Did he say why?"

They shook their heads.

"Sonofabitch," Collins said. "You ain't havin' no luck with law. Who's marshal now?"

"Ain't one."

The bartender offered, "Nobody wants the job, Sheriff."

"I see. Well, I'm puttin' a deputy at the jail. His name is Jim Zucker and he'll keep the peace."

The sheriff looked over the town, talked to some of the miners, and rode out toward the mountain in the late afternoon. He was not satisfied with Nails's answers; in fact it seemed to him that Nails considered the town to belong to him. Why had Vance Collworth picked up sticks in such a hurry? Had Nails bought out his interest in the town?

Also, it was curious that both Ned Hilton and Hickson had disappeared. That was the word the citizens had used: disappeared.

Was something very ugly going on in Eagle Rock?

He ran into one of Ramon's patrols soon after leaving the road. He was surrounded by four grim-faced men who asked his business. He showed them his badge.

"I'm the county sheriff." Collins was surprised when all four lifted their hats politely.

One said, "Will you come wi' us, Sheriff?"

They took him to the tiny Basque settlement. He got down in front of the main house. Carmelita invited him for supper.

He went inside. "I can't stay, but I'd like to talk a bit."

Ramon and Ki were away, but Carlos, Jessica, and Fernando sat with Collins while Carmelita served them coffee. Collins said, "You feel it is necessary to patrol the foothills?"

Carlos told him about the raid, and about the mysterious rider who had killed two men. "We think Nails is behind these things, Sheriff."

"Can you prove anything?"

"If we had proof, we'd have written you long ago."

"Tell me about the men who were killed."

Carlos gave him a detailed explanation of each. They had no evidence against anyone, but both men definitely were murdered.

"Because they were there," Carmelita said.

"What have you done about it?"

"We use only roving patrols now," Carlos told him. "Four men to a patrol. It will be harder for the murderer to strike again."

"If we find this person," Carmelita said, "he will have evidence on him—Esteban's knife and Pedro's belt, each with their names."

Sheriff Collins made notes on the back of an envelope. "Is Jack English here on the mountain?"

"Yes."

"I am told you busted him out of the jail."

Carlos looked surprised. "Did someone see us do that?"

"No." Collins smiled. "It is the same sort of deduction you mentioned earlier about Nails."

"We are glad he is out of jail," Carmelita said sweetly. "We thought Nails might execute him."

"He has good friends," the sheriff said, rising.

Carlos smiled. "We *are* particular about our friends."

"Where did you get the dynamite?"

Carlos spread his hands. "I have never handled dynamite in my life, Sheriff."

Collins nodded, smiling, and went out to his horse.

★

Chapter 26

Earl Miller suddenly found everything changed. The Basques were no longer in the watch-holes they had dug, but were now mounted and patrolling the foothills. All at once he felt himself on the defensive. After all, they knew these mountains from birth. Several times he had almost been detected.

He had no illusions about what would happen to him if he were caught.

The job was suddenly much less interesting—and he could see it was going to be less rewarding in money. He was not foolish enough to take on four men on their own ground. He could only win if he could hit and run.

He turned his attention from the roving guards to the little settlement. He watched it from a distance in the early evening, using binoculars, and found very little activity. There were chairs on several porches, but no one sat in them. The ground was cleared about the houses too, so to reach a porch would be a long rifle-shot. He might frighten them by shooting at windows at night, but what would that gain him? Probably nothing but a chase.

When it became dark he picketed his horse and crept close,

but all the windows were draped and he could not see in.

What if he set fire to one of the houses?

Still, Nails wanted proof of each victim. Could he tell Nails he'd shot four people running from a burning house? Nails would ask for proof.

He only had proof of two. Not a good week's work.

It began to rain as he left the vicinity of the settlement. That was another thing. Winter was coming; it was getting colder on the mountain. He sat hunched over in the saddle, letting the horse take him. Maybe he had made a bad bargain. It had sounded like easy pickings when Nails had told him about the Basques. But the reality was something else.

He made a wide detour to the east to avoid the patrols. It took hours to come out of the foothills and to cross the fields to the town, and it was very late when he arrived.

Nails had told him not to come to the Slipper, but he went there anyway. He would present his proof, get his money, and leave the town behind. The rain had tailed off by the time he reached the lowlands, but it was cold and misty.

He left his horse in front of the saloon and went inside, squinting in the sudden light. Though it was late the saloon and dance-hall were going full-blast. He realized it must be the weekend. He made his way to the bar, ordered a drink, and asked the barman for a slip of paper and a pencil. He wrote his name on the paper, folded it over, and told the barman to give it to Nails.

The bartender stared at him. "What kinda game is this?"

"Give him that paper."

Something in Miller's expression decided the barman. He nodded and Miller watched him cross the room to a door. He downed the drink and followed. In a moment the door opened and the bartender motioned him in.

Nails said, "I told you not to come here." He stood in the middle of the room, a scowl on his face.

"I'm through," Miller said. He went across to Nails's desk and tossed the knife and belt onto it.

Nails went around behind the desk and picked up the belt. "Through? You haven't even started." His tone was sarcastic. "I thought you were a better man than that."

"It's not much of a job."

"You knew about the job when you took it." Nails dropped the belt and picked up the knife. "What're these things?"

"There's names on them."

Nails sat down behind the desk. "What're you telling me?"

"I want payment for two of them Basques. Just like we agreed."

Nails shook his head. "You're a quitter, Early. You got nothing coming. Get out of here."

Miller went for his gun . . . and stopped as Nails's hand came up with a pistol. He cocked it. Nails said silkily, "I'm the law in this town. You want to challenge it?"

Miller's face was pale, his mouth a hard line. He was bursting with anger. He said throatily, "You cheatin' me, Nails."

"Get out of here."

Miller turned slowly and walked stiffly to the door. He opened it and stepped through, and slammed it.

Nails did not relax. He leaned across the desk, both hands on the big revolver, pointing at the middle of the door . . . but Miller did not open it again.

In a few moments Nails sat back, laid the pistol on the desk top, and smiled.

He picked up the leather belt, examining it curiously. He read the name burned into it on the back near the brass buckle. Pedro D. The knife had a name carefully scratched on the wooden grip: Esteban. Well, two less of the damned Basques.

Getting up, he took the belt and the knife and went out the back door to the alley. Long ago someone had built an outdoor furnace from slabs of stone. The bartenders burned trash in it daily. Nails dropped both objects into the furnace, scratched a match, and lighted wads of paper; in several minutes the fire raged, sending sparks high into the night air.

So much for Early Miller.

He had been surprised at the visit of Sheriff Collins, and he wondered what it boded. Was Collins simply making the rounds—though he had not been to Eagle Rock for years—or was the visit because of something else?

Probably he had heard complaints. Certainly there was reason for men to complain—but the sheriff would have his troubles trying to get enough evidence together to indict.

And it might be impossible for the sheriff to collect witnesses. Especially if a trial was held in Eagle Rock.

Well, the sheriff was gone now, back to his office. But he had left a deputy. That was annoying; the deputy was probably reporting constantly to Collins by telegraph.

He would have to have a talk with the deputy, size him up. Every man had his price . . . someone had said.

Days passed uneventfully; a week slipped by. Ramon found it difficult to keep the men in a high state of readiness when nothing at all was happening. The mysterious rider had not struck again, there were no more raids, no sheep killed.

Was it the calm before the storm?

When he brought them supplies, young Joseph Canfield said the town was quiet except on Saturday nights when the miners came in force from the hills to have their fun. Then there were fights and broken heads, but that was usual. The new deputy was keeping the peace.

Early Miller had left Nails's office but had not left town. He found a room in a cheap boardinghouse, giving his name as Charlie Hopkins, and went out only at night.

He scouted the Slipper, becoming familiar with the hours, and when it was closed. He had it in mind to collect from Nails in a way that Nails would not enjoy. Since Nails had cheated him out of money, then money must be important to Nails.

Early turned over several plans in his mind, and settled finally on one. He had been told the jail had been dynamited not long before, and he visualized the Golden Slipper being blown apart. It was a dream he kept coming back to. But he had no experience with blasting powder. He might easily blow himself up.

So he decided on arson. The building was weathered wood and would probably burn like a torch. Maybe Nails with it.

He bought a gallon of kerosene, and picked a good dark night.

The nights were getting cold, but the rain had let up for a week or more, so the building was dry. Several hours after the saloon closed its doors for the night, Early walked along its side, splashing kerosene on the boards.

There was a volunteer fire department in the town, but he was confident they could not save the Slipper.

He proved to be right. When he put the match flame to the oily kerosene, it flamed and ran along the side of the building in seconds. A tiny breeze helped it climb the wall, and then it began to manufacture its own wind. In minutes the entire side of the building was blazing with fire that licked into windows as glass cracked and shattered.

Miller crossed the alley behind the building and watched from half a block away, smiling at the giant bonfire he had created.

Shots were fired and people began spilling from houses. Miller joined the throng, which was kept back by the intense heat. The volunteer firemen were helpless, spraying water ineffectually.

The Slipper burned to the ground, as did four other buildings. The fire stopped at a corral, and the firemen put out the last flickers.

Nails had been in the upstairs office of the Slipper, and was not asleep when the fire started. He smelled smoke, heard the crackling, and got out at once, managing only to empty a safe and climb out a window with a gunnysack.

Several hours later one of the firemen brought him a gallon can. "I found it in the weeds near the side of the buildin' where the fire started."

Nails regarded it morosely. "So somebody started the fire?"

"It looks that way."

"Would a gallon of kerosene do it?"

"Hell, yes, with the wood all dry as tinder. With a five-minute start nobody coulda stopped it."

Nails nodded and thanked the men. So the Basques had got back at him.

Now it was war to the death.

Chapter 27

The fire was visible from the mountain, an orange torch in the night sending tongues of flame half a mile into the misty sky at its crest. It seemed as if the entire town were burning.

Ki and Ramon rode down the slopes and approached the town as the flames died and it became obvious that only a few buildings had burned—one of them the Slipper. Ramon said, "Somebody got even with Nails."

That was a possibility, Ki thought. Though houses were constantly burning down when someone knocked over an oil-filled lantern. . . .

Ramon voiced his thoughts, saying, "I wonder if Nails got out alive?"

Nails debated with himself whether to rebuild or to move on to another town. But he had roots of a sort in Eagle Rock; the saloon and dance-hall had been extremely profitable—more than anything he had yet attempted, and he was getting profit from mine shares. And the Basques had a mountain of silver. . . .

Why not rebuild? He was in an enviable position now: he'd

gotten rid of his partner, Penry, and it was his town. He had to share with no one. There was no bank in Eagle Rock; all his money was in the office safe, and he had rescued it.

For half a year he had been using a nearby store as a supply room. It had not burned, and he went there at once with the gunnysack and spent the rest of the night.

In the morning he hired men to clear the ground the Slipper had stood on, to get rid of the debris. He hired a journeyman carpenter to design a new building, and sent for building materials and men to use them.

And he spent hours planning how to attack and get rid of the Basques. They were at the root of his problems, he was positive. He sent for the new deputy, Jim Zucker, and accused the Basques of setting fire to the Slipper and the other buildings.

"They would burn the entire town if they could."

"What proof do you have, Mr. Pike?"

"I *know* they did it!"

"I can't arrest anybody on that kind of evidence. The judge would throw it out of court."

Nails tried another tack. He made his voice silky. "It would be worth a good deal to me if you would gather the evidence. I can be a generous man. . . ."

Zucker nodded. "Who in particular do you accuse?"

"The two brothers, Carlos and Ramon, the Chinaman and his woman friend—I forgot her name—and Jack English. English used to be a deputy here."

Zucker made a note of the names.

Nails said, "The brothers' father also killed one of my men, Nate Smith. I got witnesses to that, and nothing's been done to collar old Diaz."

"This is the first I've heard of it."

"Well, there's a report at the jail you can read. And you can talk to the witnesses."

"All right." Zucker made further notes. "Why did English leave here?"

"We didn't get on. He just up and quit one day."

"You've had several town marshals lately. You didn't get on with any of them?"

Nails smiled. "It's not a job that many men want. You

can't force a man to work at something if he doesn't want to. Men can make more by digging in the mines."

"I suppose so."

Jim Zucker left and inquired about Nate Smith. He had apparently been little more than a common tough and had been employed by Nails in various capacities, none of them savory. No one seemed sorry that he was no longer around.

When he talked to Harris and Link, their stories seemed to have been learned by rote. Old Fernando Diaz had knifed Smith without provocation. Zucker did not believe a word either man said.

He also learned that the Basques no longer came into the town, that Nails's men had raided into the hills, and that four men had died. There was much bad blood between Nails and the Basques.

But what he could not learn was why Nails fought the Basques. There did not seem to be a good reason.

Early Miller was delighted with his handiwork. The Slipper had burned to the ground; nothing at all was saved, according to one of the firemen he talked to. It must have cost Nails a fortune!

But it had not cost him his life.

And it had not put a penny in Miller's pockets. He had thought, when he set the fire, that he would be satisfied to see the Slipper destroyed.

But now he wanted more than that. Nails owed him money. Good hard cash. And he wanted it.

He watched the wagons come in with building materials, lumber and nails and cement, and it was no trick to watch Nails himself as he came and went. Over a period of days, Miller followed Nails to the boardinghouse where he slept, and to the store supply room, which he was using as an office.

Nails paid his workmen in cash, and he apparently had plenty of money. He certainly did not keep it at the boardinghouse . . . so it must be in the makeshift office.

Late at night Miller investigated the locks on the supply room and found them impressive. Nails was taking no chances that someone would break in. He might have to enter during the day and make a six-gun withdrawal. He'd probably have to kill Nails to do it, but that wouldn't be a great loss. In fact, he would enjoy it.

But first he'd have to case the office—see who came and went. He wanted to see Nails alone.

Watching the office proved to be less easy than he'd thought. Nails had boarded up the alley door and used only the street entrance, but to watch it Miller had to stand on the open street where anyone could see him and wonder why he was there.

There were benches and chairs in front of some stores, but none near Nails's office.

If he just picked a time and went in cold he might run into half a dozen guns. Because Nails would recognize him on sight. And, recognizing him, would probably put two and two together and realize that he, Miller, had set the fire! And start shooting.

He had to do it right the first time. Get his money and get out. It was a problem.

Though the weather had turned flukey, rain and mist one day and clear the next, Jessica could not remain indoors long. She would saddle her horse and go riding along the mountain, feeling free and unfettered.

Now and then she visited Sean Murphy at the digging. He had followed the vein along the slope, and in a series of steps had investigated its delving into the mountainside.

"After all this trouble's over, Miss Jessica, this here mine is going to be one of the richest in the country. I promise you that."

"You said once that there may be more than just silver here."

"That's right. I haven't found much gold, but there's copper in plenty." He looked worried. "Is it safe for you t'be riding out here alone?"

"Things are quiet now." She smiled at him. "And I've got a fast horse."

Jack English quickly learned that she was riding alone, and he intercepted her one misty afternoon. They walked the horses side by side and halted finally in a giant grove of pines. The ground was perfectly dry.

He helped her down in courtly fashion and they sat under the spreading branches and looked out over the valley below. It all seemed so peaceful, with no trace of hate.

She smiled when he cupped her face between his hands, tilting it up. He looked into her sea-green eyes a moment before kissing her. "I have never kissed a thief before. . . ."

It startled her. "What?"

"You have stolen my heart."

Jessie laughed. "You are a pleasant fool, Jack English." She pulled him close and kissed him . . . and sighed as he embraced her and laid her gently down. She was wearing a man's shirt, and he opened it and pressed his lips to her breasts. Her eyes fluttered and closed as she moaned softly.

In only a moment she was responding to his caresses, her sinewy body turning to him. His hand stroked the insides of her thighs and in a moment she felt his weight and opened to him, sighing again as he entered her. . . .

Beyond the shelter of the great trees it began to rain, a torrent pouring down, obliterating the valley. They were alone in the universe for those precious moments of love, and they came back slowly to reality with sighs and kisses and murmured words.

He made as if to roll away and she held him. "Don't go . . . yet."

"Of course not." His arms were around her in shared warmth. "I think I'll stay here forever."

"Forever and a day?"

"No, not that long. Just forever."

She laughed.

Chapter 28

It was no secret in Eagle Rock that Nails and the Basques were enemies. Nails had even gone so far several times as to state that he would pay a bounty for the ears of Ramon, or Carlos, or Jack English. And especially Ki and the woman, Jessica.

He was taken seriously by several who were down on their luck.

"How much bounty?" a man asked, and Nails said in front of witnesses: "One hundred dollars per ear. With proof."

A man could live for a long time on two hundred dollars.

Willie Deming thought about it. He had tried mining, but his back made it impossible. A day's digging with a shovel put him in bed for a week. He had also tried stealing and found it more lucrative but it affected his knees; they were weak.

However, he was a fair shot with a rifle. He might easily be able to snipe at one of the Basques from ambush. The thought cheered him. He bought a small pick, the kind prospectors used, and edged into the foothills far to the east. If caught he would be able to say he was merely prospecting. . . .

He had heard about the guards the Basques had instituted,

and he managed to evade them. He also discovered the caves, and made one of them his camp. But he was deathly afraid of the roving guards, and so left his horse in the caves and went on foot. A man on foot, he was positive, would have the advantage. He would be able to hear a horseman approach, and he could hide himself more easily in the underbrush.

A horseman also made a fine target.

So did a horsewoman!

He saw her first from a distance, and by the time he had made his way to the trail she followed, she had disappeared. He waited by the trail for hours, but she did not reappear.

He followed the trail west. It led him to a spot within a mile of the Basque settlement. That was too close for comfort, and he quickly retreated.

Toward evening he was nearly caught as he trudged back to the caves. Four horsemen suddenly appeared only a short distance in front of him, and he dived off the trail into a patch of sand and lay like one dead, his heart thumping like a triphammer.

But they had not seen him, and they passed by in single file. When he rose they had gone, and he sat for a time getting his breath back to normal.

That night, as he sat in one of the deep caves with a tiny Indian fire that could not be seen from outside, he wondered if this was such a good idea after all. No wonder Nails was offering so much. It was not an easy thing to do . . . but maybe he could find one of them alone. It was probably his only chance.

Ki and Jessie discussed the situation: they had come to Eagle Rock to see Vance Collworth and had discovered that "Collworth" was an impostor.

"And we're no closer to finding out what happened to him than the day we arrived," Jessie said.

Ki agreed. "But now that we know something about Nails, it's doubtful if the real Collworth is still alive."

Jessie nodded. "I'm afraid I realized that some time ago. We may never find out what happened to him." She sighed deeply. "But I'd like to know."

"So would I."

"And I don't think we can ride away and leave our friends here. They're in much danger."

"But only as long as Nails is in power. Without him, Eagle Rock would be just another town. And I agree we can't leave them, not until it's all settled."

Jessie smiled, thinking of Jack English. She had no desire to ride away and leave him, either.

When Ki left she saddled her horse and rode toward the town. The new Slipper was going up fast, built on the ashes of the old. It was easy to see from a distance. Nails was making the new one larger, too. In another month all would be as it was before, except more so.

She examined it through binoculars, the scaffolding on the building making it look much larger. Ki was right. Without Nails Eagle Rock would be just another town.

What magic could they conjure up to make Nails disappear?

Early Miller knew his days in the town were numbered. Sooner or later Nails would find out that he was hanging around. Nails liked to know everything that was going on, and people brought him information and gossip . . . some for the price of a drink.

Even with a false name, he would be turned up. So he would have to do what he planned . . . very soon.

He would do it in the morning. Nails came to the store office every morning early, after looking over the new building. Sometimes he walked through the new Slipper before the workmen started. The new building would have three floors.

Miller was sure that as soon as possible, Nails would move into his new office . . . and that time was not far off. It was another reason for haste.

Usually Nails was alone when he opened the store office. It was the obvious time to beard him in the den. He would leave his horse at the hitchrail outside the door, follow Nails in, and plug him. With the door closed, the shot should not be heard very far away. He would then scoop up what cash was available and go.

That was the bad part of the plan, but he could see no way around it. He had no idea where Nails kept his money and there was no way he could find out. There might be thousands at his elbow and he wouldn't know it. He wouldn't have much time to search for it.

On his horse, he would head out of town to the south. If there was pursuit he was certain he could lose it in the jumbled country. He had immense faith in himself out in the sticks. If he could get there.

He picked a morning and cleaned and oiled his two revolvers the night before. Nothing must go wrong.

An hour before Nails usually appeared, Early was on the street, standing in a doorway only one store away from Nails's office. His horse was at the hitchrail, a rifle in the boot and a food sack tied to the blanket roll behind the cantle. It was the only horse for a hundred yards or more in either direction, and Miller was edgy about it, but it had to be so. It was not a good plan to hurry across the wide street to his horse after he'd shot Nails. The horse had to be close by.

He was not at all nervous about what he had to do; he had lain in ambush for many others. He could see no major flaw in his plans—the presence of the horse was the weakest link. But maybe Nails would not notice. There were horses everywhere.

Nails left his horse at the livery that morning and walked the short distance to the new building. He took a great satisfaction in seeing it go up. His office would be on the top floor, twice as large as the old one, away from the noise of the dance-hall.

It had long since occurred to him that the arsonist who had set fire to the old Slipper was capable of doing the same to this new one. How could he guard against it?

He probably could not. He was positive one of the Basques had done it, so he had only one option: get rid of the Basques. But that wasn't proving to be easy.

He could hire night guards to patrol the vicinity of the building, but he could not hire an army to go into the mountains to wipe out his enemies. But he *had* to wipe them out, or push them off the land—or else give up the silver strike. If they ever discovered they were sitting on a mountain of silver . . . !

It was a huge problem.

He left the building and walked down the boardwalk toward the store office, deep in thought. As he reached for the keys to the locks, he noticed the horse. He eyed it as he unfastened the several locks. It was hitched to the rail and looked ready for travel. He could not remember another horse in that place so early.

And he could see no one around.

He opened the door and went inside, closing the door firmly. The room closest to the door had a desk and several chairs and a row of cabinets along one wall. It was his temporary office. Usually he took off his coat and seated himself behind the desk. This morning he moved to the left by the front window, where he had a tiny clear space to see the street. Most of the window had cloth tacked over it.

As he stepped close to the window he saw a shadow move to the front door. Then the door opened and a man jumped inside, his pistol leveled at the desk.

Nails drew his revolver instantly and fired. He saw a quick blur of face as the intruder jerked his head around in surprise. . . . His pistol fired and Nails sent three more shots into him as he fell.

Powder smoke swirled in the room as Nails stepped to the body. With his toe he turned it over—and was startled to see it was Early Miller.

Miller had come to kill him. Nails smiled at the other's bloody shirt. He had thought Miller long gone. Well, he was gone now.

He heard voices outside and pushed the door wide open. Max Cotton limped in. He was back on duty, though still hurting. He stared at the body on the floor. "You all right, Nails? What happened?"

"He followed me in," Nails said, indicating the body. "He thought I'd be at the desk, but I wasn't. He was a little too late."

"You know 'im?"

Nails shook his head. "Never saw 'im before."

Max knelt and pulled the dead man's head around to the light. "I seen him in town. . . ."

"Maybe some drifter lost 'is poke at the Slipper. Decided to come and get it back."

"That's prob'ly it." Max got up, grunting. "Poor, dumb shit. His luck run out all over the goddamn place."

Several men had edged into the room, with more staring in at the door. Max motioned to them. "Couple you fellers haul 'im out there to the walk. Fred, you go get a wagon."

Nails reloaded the pistol and holstered it. Max picked up the victim's gun. He opened the loading gate and turned the cylinder. "One shot fired. Went into the desk there."

Nails said, "That's prob'ly his horse out front. He was fixing to make a fast getaway."

Max nodded. "I'll take care of it." He went to the door. "Sorry 'bout all this, Nails. . . ."

"It happens," Nails growled. "Bury the sonofabitch."

★

Chapter 29

Carmelita reined in and turned in the saddle to search the backtrail. Was someone following her? She could see nothing untoward, and she heard nothing but the tiny squeaking of the saddle leather and the restless movements of the gray horse.

It must be her imagination.

She went on, walking the horse, immersed in her own thoughts. She was terribly taken with Ki; he was so many of the things she wanted in a man . . . but did they have a future together? The feud with Nails and his ilk could come between them—Ki could be killed. It was a worry that would not go away.

And yet she could not ask him to do less than her own brothers; he would resent it. And she could not send him away. No, she had to face whatever the future held.

She halted the gray again. There was a persistent sound from somewhere behind her. Her brothers had teased her when she was a girl, but it would not be like them to do it now.

She could see no one. She touched the gray's flank and

went on slowly, glancing back. Was that a movement—a hundred yards behind her?

She was dressed as a man, with a pistol about her hips. She pulled the gun, drew the hammer to half-cock, and spun the cylinder. It was fully loaded. She thought of the mysterious intruder who had killed Esteban and Pedro. Was he still lurking in the mountains? Was he following her?

The idea gave her a turn. She nudged the gray into a trot and turned down the slope at the first opportunity. It was a misty day in the mountains, with a promise of rain. She could hear someone in pursuit, paralleling her path.

When she gained the main trail she turned east instantly. The pursuer was between her and the settlement. She would have to outdistance him and circle back. She dug in her heels and the gray horse leaped ahead. She galloped for five or six minutes, bending low over the flying mane, and a glance behind showed her only the empty trail.

Maybe it was her overheated imagination after all.

She reined in slightly, loping the horse; the gray was very fast. She could probably outrun the interloper, whoever he was.

Just ahead, only a few miles, was the dry river and the miles of caves. She would circle around and come back close to the town. Glancing at the sky, she guessed the time to be late afternoon.

She moved down the slope, coming into the foothills, then across the weedy fields to the dry river. She was in the open. She reined in, halting to study her backtrail. If anyone was there, she could not spot him.

But there were plenty of places for him to hide.

She went on, curving toward the riverbed and down the gentle slope into it. It was only a dry wash now, weedy and rutted with the caves on the far side.

She felt secure in the middle of the wash, so she walked the gray, glancing about from time to time. Perhaps it had been a deer back there in the hills that had frightened her . . . or an overbold mountain lion.

She rode closer to the caves and reined in, looking at them

curiously. She hadn't been this far in ages and hadn't been inside one of the caves for years.

She did not hear the shot.

Willie Deming was above the woman when she came along. She was dressed in shirt and jeans, and her hair was tucked up into her hat. As she passed below him he was sure she was the woman with the Chinaman.

She rode a gray horse. He followed at a distance, slowing when she did, reining in when she halted. She watched the backtrail and did not search the woods above it. He knew she had heard him, but from her actions perhaps she was not sure she was followed.

He found a game trail that paralleled her route and managed to get ahead of her so that when she turned down the slope he was far ahead, still in the shelter of the trees and crossing the dry wash before she came to it. He had no plan but to stay out of her sight. She was in the open as he gained the trees above the caves, where he could look down on her.

All her attention was to the sides and rear; she halted several times to examine the area behind her. Willie smiled to himself as she began to edge closer to the caves.

He slid off the horse as she halted. Taking the Winchester, he slid closer to the rim, crawling forward on elbows and knees. Very carefully he drew a bead on her chest, at the V of her shirt, and squeezed the trigger. . . .

He did not know when the rifle fired—until the kick. He saw her jerk sideways and fall, crumpling like a rag doll in the sandy wash. The gray horse sidled away, shaking its head.

He knew a second shot was not necessary.

When Carmelita did not appear by dusk everyone became very worried. It was not like her to upset anyone. She had gone riding with the gray that afternoon, saying she felt restless.

He should have gone with her, Ki thought. He had seen her go and had started after her—but she had not asked him to accompany her and he'd thought perhaps she had reasons for being alone.

Jessica was in the main house with the others. Ki went to

the near corral and saddled his horse quickly. Mounting, he took the path he'd seen her take earlier and spurred the animal in the gathering darkness, the worry like a lump of lead in his middle. These were such troublous times . . . anything could have happened to her. He knew the others would organize a search, but he could not wait for them.

Did she have a destination, or was she just riding aimlessly? Probably the latter. The thought that she might have met the mysterious killer was strong in his mind. His hand felt for the *shuriken* concealed in his vest. But the steel was cold to his touch.

She had been gone for hours . . . how far had she ridden? She might have turned off anywhere and not followed this path at all.

There were too many ifs.

In half an hour it was full dark and he reined in, sitting the horse, listening to the silence around him. Was he on a fool's errand? She might have returned to the house minutes after he had left it.

He went on at a walk, wondering if he should go back. In the morning they might find tracks—or some clue. It was so dark now he could barely make out the trail. And yet he could not make himself turn back. He had a feeling—he could not explain—that she was out here somewhere.

After a long while the trail petered out. He turned back and headed down the slope after a mile or so and came to the open. He crossed rutted fields and came finally to the dry wash. Wasn't this where the caves were?

But why would Carmelita have gone to the caves? Probably she had not.

He halted in the middle of the wide wash, listening. From far off a coyote barked, a lonesome sound. Away to his right an owl hooted at intervals, probably out hunting. He studied the sky, getting his bearings. The town was far away to his left.

He could think of no reason why she would go there.

Maybe the best thing would be to make a circle and head back to the settlement. There was very little he could do in the dark.

He started south, and a short while later his horse nickered.

Something moved a hundred yards or so to his right. It was a wraith-like shape and Ki slid a *shuriken* into his hand and turned toward it.

In another moment he saw it was a riderless horse. Carmelita's gray! The animal was saddled, reins trailing. . . . Where was she?

★

Chapter 30

He got down and examined the gray. The animal was unhurt but nervous. Had Carmelita dismounted and the horse run off? Wasn't that very unlikely?

He mounted again, with the reins of the gray in his hand, and walked toward the caves, intending to make a circle about the place he'd first seen the gray horse. . . . A sense of foreboding reached into his heart.

And then he saw her.

He jumped down and ran to the crumpled body, turning her over slowly. Carmelita was facedown in the sand, dead from a shot that had drilled through the center of her chest. Already the body was cooling.

Instinctively Ki raised his eyes to the cliff above the caves. Probably the shot had come from there.

He felt a deep anger flooding him. What kind of man would ambush a young woman? Was it someone hired by Nails? He laid her out straight, arms by her sides, tears gathering in his eyes. She had been so alive . . . so beautiful . . .

For a moment he debated carrying her back to the settlement. But many of them would be out searching for her. He looked about and began to pick up sticks and twigs. In a few moments he had a small pile; he made a teepee of dry twigs and struck a match. The fire curled around the twigs and smoke rose quickly. In minutes he had a fire and was adding to it.

In five minutes he had a bonfire. It kept him busy finding brush and driftwood. Sparks rose hundreds of feet into the air: a signal fire that could not be ignored.

In half an hour he heard the first hoofbeats . . . then Ramon materialized from the gloom at the head of five men. "What is it?"

Ki said nothing. Ramon flung himself off the horse and ran to the body, kneeling by it. When he looked up at Ki there were tears on his cheeks. "You saw no one?"

Ki shook his head. He pointed to the cliff. "I think it came from up there. When it's light I'll go up and look for tracks."

"I'll go with you."

"No. You must take her back. See that it is done properly. I'll stay here in one of the caves tonight."

Ramon sighed, nodding. "Very well."

Several of the men had blanket rolls. They made a sling, wrapping the body tenderly. They carried it between two horsemen. When they had gone, Ki allowed the fire to die out. He rode to the caves and bedded down for the remainder of the night. What a terrible day it had been. . . .

He could not sleep, but toward morning he dozed a bit, waking with the first tentative rays of the weak sun. Saddling the horse at once, he rode south, following the bends of the dry river until he found a place where he could climb the crumbling cliff to the flatland above.

When he reached a place opposite the ashes of last night's bonfire, he dismounted and looked for signs, finding them at once. A man had tied his horse here . . . had crawled on hands and knees close to the rim, here. And in the weeds was a shell casing, a .44 Winchester. A bit of brass that had contained the powder and bullet that had snuffed out Carmelita's life.

He tucked it into a pocket.

Following the tracks was easy. The ground was not dust-dry; it had been misty and the nights were even more so. The tracks led north, following the winding riverbed until they went down the low cliff as the riverbed widened and the cliffs petered out.

The tracks led toward the town. In one particular stretch of wet, soft sand, the killer's horse left excellent impressions. The left front shoe was well worn and had a gouge at the toe. If he saw it again, he would know it.

He lost the tracks a mile or so from the town. They turned into a well traveled road and were trampled out by other horses and wagons.

It was too early in the day to go into the town with any hope that he would not be recognized. He left the road and headed toward the mountains, sure now that Nails had employed a bushwhacker. What other explanation could there be? A bushwhacker who would kill anyone he saw.

Ki gritted his teeth. What would he give for a chance at a man like that!

He had gone several miles when he met the three men. They immediately spread out, rifles on him. Ki halted. "What is it you want?"

"You're headin' toward the mountains."

Ki gestured vaguely. "I've got a claim. Why do you care where I go?"

One of the men said, "I've seen you b'fore. You're the feller killed Nate Smith with a knife."

Ki shrugged. "Who's Nate Smith?"

"He's the feller, all right. I told you he was a Chinaman, didn't I? Well, this's him. Nails'll pay us a bounty for him."

Ki looked them over carefully. They were dressed in rough clothes, all armed with pistols and rifles. The man who had spoken looked familiar. Maybe he was the one Jessie had shot in the leg. He said, "I never saw you before."

The other grinned. "That's horseshit. I seen *you*." He cocked his rifle. "Watch him, Fred. He quicker'n a goddamn rattler."

The man called Fred nudged his horse closer and exchanged his rifle for a pistol. "Put your hands up high."

Ki raised his hands.

Fred came close, the revolver ready. He patted Ki's vest, found the knife, and held it up. "He ain't got a gun."

"That's the knife he killed Nate with."

Fred touched the *shuriken*. "What's them things?"

"Decorations," Ki said.

Fred nodded and backed his horse. "We taken you into town." He smiled at the others. "He oughta be worth somethin' to Nails."

"Nails'll cut his heart out."

Fred poked him with the muzzle of the pistol. "Get going."

Ki reached out. The flat of his hand cut down on Fred's wrist in a lightning chop. The pistol spun away. He heard a rifle shot as he spurred the horse, and he hurled a *shuriken* at the man in front of him. The shot went wild as the star tore out the man's throat. The third man stared, mouth open, seemingly shocked into immobility. He saw the dead man's blood pouring in a torrent, and he fired his rifle over Ki's head, turned his horse, and spurred frantically.

Ki let him go.

Fred had jerked his rifle from the scabbard, but got no farther than cocking it when a second throwing star struck him and hurled him from the saddle.

It had happened in seconds. Ki got down and retrieved his weapons, wiping them clean on Fred's shirt. He hadn't wanted to kill these fools, but he could not let them take him into town where Nails would surely have him hanged . . . or worse.

He examined the shoes on both horses; neither was the one he sought.

He looked at the tracks of the third horse. It had not been at the caves, either. Mounting, he rode on to the mountain.

There was a small graveyard on the mountain, and a man was digging a grave as Ki returned to a house, full of gloom. Carmelita's death was a heavy burden to her parents; her mother was abed and Fernando sat by her, holding her hand.

Ramon was of a mind to burn down the entire town, and had to be reminded that their good friends the Canfields lived there and would lose everything.

Jessie said, "We must report the murder to the sheriff. It may cause him to take action."

"Nothing will make him take action," Ramon growled.

• • •

Nails would not see Willie Deming. One of his bartenders reported to him that Willie was in the bar, demanding to see Nails on a matter of importance.

"What importance?" Nails asked. "I don't know anybody by that name."

"He won't say."

"What does he look like?"

"He's a saddle bum if you ask me. He probably wants money."

Nails grunted. "Does he think I hand out money to bums? Get rid of him." He waved the barman out.

With that answer, Willie sat at a table, sipping beer. So Nails wouldn't pay up as he'd said. He looked around the fine new saloon, resplendent with fine colors and gaudy lanterns. The entire place had burned to the ground not long ago.

It crossed Willie's mind that it could burn again.

And the more he drank the better it sounded. Nails, the sonofabitch, had cheated him—wouldn't even see him, and here he'd gone and shot that Basque woman for him.

He got out a wooden match and stared at it. All this fine palace would go up in smoke again. That would show Nails. That would show him to fool around with Willie Deming.

He had another beer.

Chapter 31

Duddy Rintel raced into town and reined in at the marshal's office. Max Cotton was in, dozing at his desk, but he woke when Duddy yelled, "That Chinaman! He got Link and Fred! Knifed them both!"

Max got to his feet. "The Chinaman? Where was this?"

"Outside of town . . . over by the crick."

Max looked him over. "You all right?"

"I got away. He killed 'em both!"

"You seen it?"

"Sure I seen it! Ain't you goin'—?"

Max waved his hand. "Calm down, for Crissakes. Tell me what happened. Where'd you meet this here Chinaman?"

"I tole you, over by the crick. We was comin' in and he just showed up. Fred said let's take 'im in to Nails . . . get a bounty. We was holding rifles on him and Fred pulled 'is pistol. Then the Chinaman knocked the pistol away and threw a knife at Link."

"And what was you doing all this time?"

"Lissen, goddammit! It all happened so damned fast! The Chinaman, he didn't have a gun. Fred took 'is knife—"

"I thought you said he knifed Link!"

Duddy frowned. "He musta had a couple knives. Anyways, he threw a knife at Link and I fired at him. Then m'horse jumped and skittered—the shot musta spooked him. I looked back and saw Fred fall offen his nag."

Max shook his head. "So three of you couldn't handle him, izzat right?"

Duddy growled, "You never seen anybody so fast."

"You said he didn't have no gun."

"He didn't *need* no gun."

"All right. Lemme get my horse."

With Duddy leading, Max rode to the spot and got down to kneel by the two bodies. Each had his throat torn out; there was much blood.

He looked at Duddy. "These here wounds wasn't made by no knife."

"The hell they wasn't! I seen it hit Link!"

"Did it look like a knife?"

"It was a goddamn flash of steel, that's what I saw!"

Max rose, shaking his head. "I never seen a knife-wound like these here two." He motioned. "Bring them horses over here. We'll take the bodies into town."

When Max reported to Nails that two more men were dead, Nails was disgusted and demanded to know details.

"That Chinaman again!"

"Duddy says he knifed both of them."

"What did Duddy do?"

"He ran like a scared chicken."

Nails grunted. "Then maybe you can't believe anything he says."

Nails stared at the opposite wall after Max had gone. The problem of how to get the damned Basques off the mountain seemed to loom larger every time he thought about it.

Willie Deming sat in the Alamo Saloon till closing, then stumbled out into the chill air and looked at the misty sky. No stars; it smelled like rain.

He climbed on his horse and walked to the end of town. Eagle Rock was a two-bit little burg and there was no future for him here. Why not get out tonight? He rolled a brown cigarette and put it in the corner of his mouth. He scratched a wooden match on the saddle horn and looked at the yellow glow of it. He let it burn down almost to his fingers before he lit the cigarette.

He turned the horse and looked toward the Slipper. Why not tonight? He could set fire to the saloon and be miles down the road while it burned.

Grinning at the idea, he walked the horse back into town. No one was on the street. The Slipper was closed... everything in town was closed. He left the horse tied alongside a heavy wagon and walked slowly toward the Slipper.

There was a passageway between buildings and he turned into it to the back of the row where the sheds and privies were. All was silent except for a dog baying in the distance. Slowly he approached the back of the Slipper. It was the tallest building in town, looming over him.

He felt the side of it—rough boards. It would take a good fire to get them started. He looked around for kindling and noticed a trash barrel. It was full of paper and cardboard. Just the thing! He lugged it to the side of the building and set it down with a thump.

Then he paused, listening. Was that a sound from the far side of the privies?

It did not come again, so he pulled paper from the barrel and wadded it up. There ought to be enough kindling in the barrel to get the boards started.

He scratched a match and leaned in to light the paper.

As he did so he heard the hoofbeats. Someone was approaching along the alley. The paper flared up and a voice yelled, calling a name.

Willie scuttled away as a shot was fired in the air. He ducked into the space between the buildings and ran out to the street. The fire had blazed up four or five feet above the barrel. Maybe it had got a good start and they wouldn't be able to put it out!

He threw himself at the horse and dug in his heels, racing for the south end of town. Someone fired three shots behind him. He heard a bell start to ring.

He had a good start and a fast horse. But they were coming. He glanced behind as he left the last of the dark buildings and entered the rutted trail that led around the mountain. He could make out a group of horsemen. Well, he'd soon leave them behind. Someone fired a rifle, and at once he heard the zing as a bullet sped by a little too close.

In a few minutes he turned off the road. They were coming too fast. He'd have to lose himself in the trees. They couldn't track him at night. He halted the horse in a copse and in a few moments they went by him, half a dozen, strung out along the dim trail.

He looked toward the town and could see no fire. Damn! Maybe they had put it out. He hadn't had enough time to get it started properly.

But he couldn't stay here. He nudged the horse and turned east. He'd circled the town and head north instead. Let them search the other way. He walked the animal slowly through the trees, picking his way.

Then he reined in suddenly. There were hoofbeats in front of him, a little to the right. Jesus! Had they circled back?

He turned to the left and dug in his heels. Someone yelled at him to halt. Willie twisted in the saddle and fired his revolver in the direction of the voice.

Someone shouted, and a half-dozen shots clipped the bark from trees near him. He fired again, then leaned low over the horse's back, swearing. The bastards had come on him by luck! Now he'd have to outrace them.

He never felt the shot that tumbled him from the saddle. He was dead before he touched the ground.

Four men came up and reined in. One struck a match as Ramon got down and turned the body over. Sightless eyes stared at the gloomy sky.

"Anybody know 'im?"

No one did.

But the next morning Ki looked at the man's horse. The left front shoe made the same imprint he'd seen in the wet sand. This was the man who had killed Carmelita.

Ramon had the body buried on the flats, off their land. They did not bother to mark the grave.

Chapter 32

A short, dapper little man wearing a checked suit under a gray duster appeared, driving a black buggy. He stopped in front of the Golden Slipper, got out and tacked a crude poster to the wall, then went inside for a drink.

The poster drew a small crowd who gawked at it.

> CIRCUIT JUDGE WILL BE IN EAGLE ROCK ON THURSDAY NEXT. COURT WILL BE HELD FOR ONE TO THREE DAYS. HIS HONOR FRANK BAILEY, PRESIDING.

There was a scrawled signature which could not be read. The man in the duster said his name was Chester Shopwin. "Get your cases ready," he said to one and all. "First come, first served."

He went out to his buggy and drove on.

Young Joseph Canfield brought the news to Ramon. A judge was coming to town! Maybe now their troubles with Nails would come to an end.

Jessica said, "Don't get your hopes up too high."

"He'll have to listen to us," Ramon retorted. "You can't sweep murder under the rug!"

"But lawyers can twist facts. Is there a lawyer in Eagle Rock?"

"Yes, but he's in Nails's pay."

Frank Bailey was forty-six; he had been a judge for five years. At the age of twenty-three he had worked in a law office in Ohio as a clerk. Two years later he was in Denver, also as a clerk. But the following year he had been certified to be of good moral character, had passed a cursory examination, and was given a certificate that allowed him to hang up his own shingle.

There were too many lawyers in Denver, and some had actually been through law school. Bailey moved farther west, eking out a living, until he met Hiram Biggs, a wealthy cattleman. He was able to save Biggs a good deal of money in a land case. Several homesteaders had fenced a spring that was essential to Biggs's ranch. Bailey discovered, in Biggs's papers, a prior claim to the land, and it was settled in Biggs's favor.

Biggs appreciated the "discovery," and when, several years later, the circuit judge died, he was able to get Bailey appointed to the post. He never regretted it.

Bailey flourished as judge. It was whispered that a poor man up against a rich one had no chance in Bailey's court, but nothing could be proved.

Bailey had no desire to travel to Eagle Rock; he was comfortable in his large house in Kimberly, and Eagle Rock was far out of his usual circuit. But Sheriff Collins insisted that all was not as it should be in that town, that it would not be the worse for a good dose of law.

So, reluctantly, Bailey packed up, changed his schedule, and climbed into his big, closed buggy driven by his usual black servant, Jules.

It was a long, wearying trip, and he arrived tired out and grumpy on Wednesday night. He put up at the Granger House, demanding the best rooms they had. Jules saw to it that a bathtub was carried upstairs and hot water provided.

Nails came to see him that night after supper. The two had

drinks in Bailey's rooms, served by Jules. They got on famously.

On Thursday morning Bailey slept late. Then, half a day was spent rearranging the Slipper to his taste, setting it up as a courtroom. Most of the town wished to attend—court trials were almost as good an entertainment as a hanging. But there was room for only about sixty persons, with tables and chairs set apart for the judge, attorneys, and witnesses.

Though the town had only one attorney.

The judge took a long lunch and reappeared at two in the afternoon carrying a satchel which contained his judicial robe, certain papers, and a bible. Bailey had long since learned that small towns could not be depended upon to contain even one Good Book—unless of course there happened to be a clergyman or a church, which was not likely.

The few remaining hours of the day were spent disposing of small cases.

The next day more small cases were brought him, and Bailey disposed of one after another, adjudicating problems, imposing fines, and delivering several stern lectures. He considered it part of his duty to explain the law now and then, though his interpretation of it would certainly have awed an Eastern law professor, as it did his bucolic audience.

On Court Day Ramon, Carlos, Ki, and Jessica came to town, well armed, and managed seats in the Slipper. The judge had appointed a temporary clerk and Ramon handed him a sheet of foolscap which enumerated the Basque case against Nails.

Their case was not called the first day. Nor the second.

On the third day Judge Bailey read the particulars as Ramon had set them out, and asked Ramon to take the witness chair.

The clerk asked him, "What is your name?"

"Ramon Diaz."

"Put your hand on the bible. Do you swear t'tell the whole truth?"

"Yes, I do."

The clerk resumed his seat and the judge asked, "Where is

your proof, Diaz? You list a lot of charges here, but can you prove anything at all?"

"I didn't think it was up to me to prove anything, Judge. Isn't that what the law is supposed to do?"

"Up to a point, yes. But you accuse Mr. Pike of murdering your sister, Carmelita." The judge waved the paper. "You say here that he hired someone to do it."

Ramon asked, "Who's Mr. Pike?"

"You know him as Nails."

"Well, Your Honor, we found the man who shot my sister—"

"Is he in the courtroom?"

Ramon shook his head. "He's dead."

"And did he say in front of witnesses, before he died, that Mr. Pike had hired him to kill your sister?"

"No, he didn't say anything. We were chasing him and he fired at us."

"I see. Are you saying you murdered *him?*"

"It was a fair fight, Your Honor. We tried to capture him and he didn't want it that way."

"So actually you cannot prove Mr. Pike hired him."

Ramon stared at the judge. "That means that Nails can go on hiring people to kill us, is that right?"

Bailey pointed a finger at him. "You are mighty close to contempt of court, sir."

Ramon shrugged. "I'm telling you the truth. The man who murdered my sister didn't even know her—probably never saw her before. He came into the mountains to kill as many of us as he could. Somebody paid him to do it."

"But there is no proof who that somebody is."

"Only one man would profit by it."

"Nevertheless, you have no proof." Bailey rapped sharply with his gavel. "Case dismissed."

The clerk motioned to Ramon, who rose, stared at the judge, and went back to his seat beside Ki. He sat fuming until the end of the day's proceedings.

As they filed out of the saloon five men surrounded Ki with drawn guns and Max Cotton said, "You're under arrest, mister."

They pulled Ki out of the crowd, holding off Ramon and Carlos.

"What's the charge?" Ki asked.

"You kilt Nate Smith . . . and now we got a judge here, you gonna hang for it."

★

Chapter 33

They put Ki in the reconstructed jail, and two men were constantly on guard inside and two outside. He would be tried the next day.

"There isn't time to break him out," Jack English said that night. "We'd need a good plan. They're guarding him too closely."

"Maybe we can rescue him when they take him from the jail to the saloon," Ramon suggested.

Jessie shook her head. "There'll be just as many guards."

"They're going to find him guilty," Carlos said. "That judge is in Nails's pay for sure. Where will they take Ki to hang him?"

"Probably outside of town," Ramon said, pulling at his nose. "Maybe those oaks at the north end."

"That's our best bet," Jack said. "How many men can we depend on?"

"At least ten. With fast horses."

"That ought to be enough. We make a hell of a lot of noise, grab Ki, and run for the hills." Jack grinned at them. "And with any luck we might puncture Nails."

Carlos's prediction seemed to be coming true. The next day Ki was put on trial for the killing of Nathan Smith. He was sworn in and took the chair to the right of the judge's table.

There was one witness—Johnny Harris. He had shaved and the whiskers were gone, but he was the same mean-looking hombre Ki and Jessie had faced that day on the trail when they had rescued Fernando Diaz.

"Tell the court what happened," the attorney said to him. "In your own words."

Harris nodded, not looking at Ki. "Me and Link and Nate, we was riding along, coming toward town, when we met the Chinaman and that there girl." He pointed to Jessica. "When we got close to 'em, the Chinaman just up and thrown some kinda knife at Nate. Knocked 'im off the horse, dead."

"That's a lie," Ki said. "It didn't happen that way."

Judge Bailey rapped his gavel. "I d'want any talk from you."

"Don't you want the truth?"

"We'll get at the truth." Bailey looked at the lawyer. "Go on."

The lawyer motioned to Harris, who said, "Then the woman there, she shot Link in the leg."

"Go on."

"Well, that's all there was to it. I put Nate's body on 'is horse and we went into town. Link went to see Doc Hamblin and I took Nate to the undertaker's."

The lawyer indicated Ki. "And you never saw this man before?"

"No sir, never."

"Then why did he kill Nate?"

"I figgered they had something between them that I didn't know about."

"You mean bad blood?"

Harris nodded. "Nate said something about 'there's that Chinaman again.' Then he knifed Nate."

"I see." The lawyer turned to Bailey. "This is an obvious case of murder, Your Honor."

"Do I get a chance to speak now?" Ki asked.

Bailey looked at him. "What is it you wish to say?"

"What this man has told you is mostly untrue. We met him

and two others on the road, but they were not alone. They were beating an old man—"

"That's a goddamn lie!" Harris yelled.

"I have a witness," Ki said. "Jessica Starbuck." He pointed to her.

The lawyer said, "I am told those two are a team, Your Honor. They will naturally corroborate each other."

Bailey nodded. "Yes, I understand."

Ki said, "The man they were beating was Fernando Diaz. His two sons are in this room."

Ramon and Carlos got up, and Judge Bailey pounded with the gavel. "Order, please." He frowned at the brothers. "Were you two present at the altercation in the road?"

"No." Ramon shook his head. "But our father was brought home—"

"Then you are not a witness."

"—was brought home very badly beaten."

Bailey rapped. "Please sit down."

Jessica rose. "But I am a witness, Your Honor. I was a part of that—"

"You have not been sworn. Come forward, young woman."

Jessica moved toward the clerk who held out a bible. She put her hand on it and swore to tell the truth. She was directed to the witness chair.

The attorney asked, "You are close friends with this man?" He pointed to Ki.

"Yes."

"What is your version of the affair we are discussing?"

"When Ki and I came along the road we found this man" —she indicated Harris—"and two others beating Mr. Diaz. They attacked us immediately."

"She's a liar!" Harris yelled.

The judge rapped hard. "That's enough of that." He laid the gavel down. "Is Fernando Diaz in the courtroom?"

"No, Your Honor."

"I see." Bailey turned to Jessica. "And what happened when you say you were attacked?"

"Ki was forced to kill one of them. I had to shoot another in the leg."

"In the leg?"

"I did not want to kill him, Your Honor. Then we forced them to go into the town. Ki and I took Mr. Diaz to his home."

The judge looked at Harris. "Where is the man who was shot in the leg?"

"He was killed, Your Honor," Harris replied. "We think them Basques did it."

"And you were not beating this old man?"

"Hell no—I mean, no sir. That's a lie."

There was a stir from the audience and the judge rapped sharply. "Quiet—quiet." He pointed to Jessica. "You're excused, ma'am."

Jessica resumed her seat in the audience.

Judge Bailey frowned at his notes. "It is the opinion of this court that, inasmuch as we have conflicting testimony, and that the witness, Jessica Starbuck, admits this man, Ki, killed Mr. Smith, that Ki be found guilty."

He rapped again as a loud murmur arose. "Sentence will be handed down at a later date. Take the prisoner away." He got up and rapped again. "Court is adjourned."

Max Cotton and two others gathered around Ki. The people of the audience began to shuffle out of the room into the street. As Ki was led through the door a number of men in the street began to yell, "Hang him! Hang him! Hang the bastard!"

Someone swung a rope.

A dozen men surged toward Ki. Max pulled a pistol and was immediately knocked to the ground. The other deputies were overpowered and disarmed. Ki was hustled to a hitchrail and put on a horse. Surrounded by men, some of whom began to fire pistols into the air, Ki galloped out of town.

Mounting her own horse, Jessie followed quickly.

As she caught up to them, several of the men were laughing, yelling, "Hang him!"

Ramon and Carlos fired into the air and Ki grinned. It was a very successful necktie party.

Nails was furious. "You let the sonofabitch get away! You had him right here and you let him get the hell away!"

“Dammit, Nails, there were a dozen of ’em!” Max had a bandage on his forehead and splashes of blood on his torn shirt.

“But you’re the goddamn law!”

“Only if I got the most guns. They coulda killed me out there.”

“All right. Get outta here.” Nails pointed to the door. He slumped behind the desk. What good was the judge to him? Maybe it was a mistake to go after the Basques one by one . . . but how else could it be done? He couldn’t attack their land.

He got up and paced the office. No, he couldn’t attack the land. But—what about their right to the land? He pounded one fist into the other. What about their deed? If he could prove that was no good, he’d have them in a squeeze! And this was something the judge could help with.

He opened the door and yelled for Judge Bailey.

Chapter 34

Homer Gregg's appointment with the U.S. marshal in Belmer was for eleven o'clock. The lettering on the door read: GAGE COLEMAN, UNITED STATES MARSHAL. At ten minutes past the hour the door opened and a dumpy, short man with thick glasses beckoned to him.

"Mr. Coleman will see you now, sir."

Gregg was dressed in a conservative gray suit; he carried a leather folder with an inch-thick sheaf of papers inside. He smiled as the marshal came round the desk to shake hands.

"Good morning."

"Good morning, Marshal. As I told you in my letter, I've come about Eagle Rock—or perhaps more to the point, about Harry Pike, the man they call Nails."

Coleman leaned back in his chair. He had the letter before him. "You say here that you believe Vance Collworth is dead?"

"Yes. The circumstances of his departure from the town are bizarre, if we are to take the word of Nails. I have not been able to turn up any trace of the man. He did not board any stage in either Eagle Rock or any town within a hundred miles on the day that Nails says he left."

"Still, it is possible—"

"Collworth was not an outdoor man, sir. He was totally unused to sleeping in the open, and there is no reason that I can discover why he would slip out of town secretly. It was common knowledge, my informants tell me, that Nails and Collworth did not get along well."

"I see. And you also state that Collworth was not his real name."

"His real name was Thurston Penry. He assumed the name Collworth when he arrived in Eagle Rock. He also assumed the person of the real Collworth . . . inasmuch as he resembled him. The real Collworth disappeared completely. I am certain he was killed and buried—just as I am certain Nails killed and buried Penry."

"You are saying this Nails person solved his problems by killing."

"Exactly, sir. All this is more or less corroborated by the Ned Hilton notes which I sent you."

"Yes, I read them with interest."

"And I have other documents here. . . ." Gregg pulled them from the folder. "I had three other informants in the town besides Jack English, and they support one another in the facts. In my opinion there is more than enough to indict Harry Pike."

Coleman nodded. "My legal assistants tell me the same." He glanced at the papers Gregg gave him. "I'll have my staff go over these. What is the situation in Eagle Rock now?"

"There is a circuit judge there at the moment."

"Do you mean Bailey?"

"Yes."

The marshal sighed.

Gregg said, "He is not a credit to the profession, sir."

"I know." Coleman nodded. "I am doing what I can to have him removed from office. I believe I will succeed." He rose and came round the desk again, holding out his hand. "I must congratulate you on your thorough work, Mr. Gregg. It is much appreciated."

"I rather enjoyed it, sir. It's not often an attorney gets to play detective."

"I'm certain your employers are pleased."

Gregg smiled. "They say they are." He picked up his leather folder and went to the door.

The trial of Ki, and the judge's subsequent guilty verdict, was a great disappointment to the Basque community. It meant that justice had departed Eagle Rock, possibly for good.

And Nails had won. With the backing of the law, and considering himself above the law, what might he do next?

Young Joseph reported that hard-bitten men were drifting into town, possibly drawn by offers of jobs by Nails.

Was another raid in the making? Ramon was certain of it. He was tireless in his patrols, and even sent men into the town at night to look and listen. Ki was one of them.

But Nails had been paying for information for years, and the news of the Basques' night-time expeditions had spread. One of Marshal Coleman's clerks heard office talk of impending action. He told his wife that something important was about to happen that would probably affect Eagle Rock. His wife's sister was married to a miner who worked in that vicinity, and she relayed the suspicions to him.

He immediately sold the information to Nails, who became very disturbed. The U.S. marshal, about to take action in Eagle Rock?

He paced the office thinking about it. If the marshal had solid evidence he would probably move in with troops, maybe cavalry from the nearest army post. The marshal would also bring his own law, doubtless a district judge.

If that happened, it was all up. If the U.S. marshal moved it meant he had hard, irrefutable evidence.

How much time did he have? Maybe only hours. Nails emptied the safe and changed his clothes; it was but a few hours till dark. He hated to wait, but he must not be seen leaving town. He took up a vigil at a small window at the front of the building, where he could see the entire street. It was likely that if the marshal entered with troops it would be early in the morning.

If so he would have hours to put distance between himself and them. He would head south, then bend east and wind up in New Orleans, a very long way from Colorado.

It was time to relax and enjoy some of the money he'd accumulated . . . in a way that Eagle Rock could not provide.

No troopers entered the town before dark.

He was certain that meant they would not show up until morning at the earliest. He had a large supper sent upstairs to his office and ate only half of it. He would take the other half with him.

Saying nothing to anyone, he went down the back stairs to the stable. Leaving Eagle Rock meant he was leaving thousands of dollars behind—the building itself and all its future profits. But it could not be helped if he were to stay out of a federal penitentiary.

He saddled a gray horse, tied on his money sack and the food, shoved a rifle in the boot, and led the animal out to the alley, seeing no one.

It was a wrench to leave; the town had been a gold mine to him, far more than he'd anticipated. Part of it was because of Thurston Penry who had fronted for them for a time . . . until his damned demands. Well, it had got Penry nothing but the same kind of grave the real Collworth had been pushed into. Too bad.

Nails mounted the gray and walked the animal along the rear of the buildings in deep shadow.

At the end of the rutted alley he turned into the road and headed south past the shacks and tents that had sprung up at the end of the town.

He did not notice the rider who halted his horse and peered at him from the shelter of a mud-caulked hut.

Nails tugged his coat collar closer against the chill wind and nudged the gray into a lope. By morning he would be miles away, probably too far for a posse or troopers to find or catch him. How would they know in which direction to search?

He would simply have disappeared.

★

Chapter 35

Ki nudged the horse and stepped out from behind the hut, staring after the disappearing rider. It was Nails! He was positive. What was Nails doing in the middle of the night, hightailing it out of town? There was a blanket roll behind the cantle and a warbag tied to his pommel—was Nails getting out?

Had he heard news that had not yet reached the mountains?

It looked like it. Ki spurred after the departing rider, staying far back. There was no way to warn any of the others; he would have to follow Nails himself. And bring him back.

The road wound between hills, only a two-cart track in most places. A light drizzle greeted him after an hour, and Ki shrugged into a dark slicker. He had no blanket roll or food, not expecting a prolonged chase. He hoped it would not be long. . . .

Toward morning it began to rain. He had not seen the man he pursued, but the tracks were plain in the light mud of the trail. Nails was only a few minutes ahead of him.

As it became light, Ki walked his horse warily, expecting Nails to halt. The chances were that Nails would halt and eat something, perhaps even build a small fire and boil coffee.

But he did not. Several times Ki glimpsed him, a hunched-over figure on a gray horse, moving steadily.

More than ever now, Ki was convinced that Nails was trying to put as many miles behind him as possible. He was probably carrying a large amount of money, intent on putting this part of the country out of his mind. Maybe heading for Mexico.

How would he stop Nails?

He could not just ride up to the man—in this lonely country Nails would never permit it. His rifle would come out of the boot and there would be a battle. Nails had too much to lose.

Would Nails stop at the next town? Probably not, if it had a telegraph. If Nails was running from the law—maybe Sheriff Collins had come to town to arrest him—then a "wanted" order would go out by wire.

Maybe his best bet would be to get ahead of Nails and ambush him, force him to give up. But that wouldn't be easy either.

The rain continued, a steady downpour, hour after hour, and the trail became a quagmire. Still Nails continued doggedly, head bowed. Ki had no choice but to follow.

At midday the rain let up for a bit. They were in a deep canyon where a rain-swollen stream surged and frothed beside the trail. Unexpectedly Nails halted there, and Ki nearly rounded a bend in sight of him, but managed to pull back. Nails halted for half an hour, then went on.

In the middle of the afternoon the rain began again, and toward evening they came to a cross trail. Nails immediately turned east.

They had come out of the hills and were in a wide, flat plain that was nearly treeless. The trail led straight east, a dark trace on the yellow-brown earth. Nails was not in sight.

Ki hesitated. When he crossed this flat area he would be at Nails's mercy—if Nails was waiting for him in the trees, a mile or so away. He had thought earlier about ambushing Nails—and here was a perfect place for Nails to do the same to him.

But the tracks led eastward. Ki took a deep breath and

followed. He would not hear or feel the bullet that hit him.

Nails was not waiting for him.

He passed through a small forest of pines and before him was a tiny settlement, four houses with yellow lantern-light glimmering from their windows. Ki sat the horse and peered at it. It was probably a store and a post office.

It was too dark to see if Nails's gray was at one of the hitchrails. But he had to know.

He got down, tied the horse, and slogged through the mud to a row of saplings. It was raining only lightly, pattering down as he moved to the side of the first house. It was a heavy log hut, cold as ice to the touch. He moved around it and saw that all four houses were arranged haphazardly with no semblance of a street. He could see no telegraph wire; it was very unlikely that a wire would be strung to this tiny cluster in the middle of nowhere.

There was a gray horse standing three-legged at a hitchrail.

He crossed to the horse, seeing no one. Every house was shut up tight except the one where the horse waited. It had a sign: GEN'L STORE. It was probably the reason for the town. There was a blanket roll behind the cantle. Nails's horse.

There was a porch, two steps up, and Ki went up softly and peered in the nearest window, but it was so grimed he could see nothing inside. The second window was the same.

The door had a knob. He turned it. The door was not locked. Nails was undoubtedly inside, warming himself at the stove. Smoke was coming from the chimneys of all four houses. If he walked inside would Nails recognize him instantly?

If so, he would start shooting, knowing he was pursued.

Maybe the store had a back door.

Ki stepped off the little porch and slogged around to the back of the building. The rain had turned to a fine mist. He grasped the knob of the back door but it would not turn. It was locked.

He went back to the front. Should he wait till Nails came out? If he went inside now he would be at a great disadvantage. Nails could be anywhere in the room, behind anything.

As he was debating the matter, the door opened and Nails came out.

They were six feet apart and Nails's pistol was in his hand instantly, pointing at Ki's middle. He had come from the store with the gun in his hand, Ki realized.

But he was surprised to see Ki. "You're that damned Chinaman!"

"Half Japanese," Ki said.

"What the hell are you—you're following me!"

Ki took a guess. "You're wanted by the law."

Nails smiled. "Are you the law, then? Or are you a bounty hunter?" He motioned with the pistol. "Drop your knife on the ground. Do it real easy."

Ki pulled the throwing knife with two fingers and dropped it as ordered, his face expressionless. The point stuck in the wood and quivered.

"Back up." Nails picked up the knife.

Ki stepped down the stairs to the muddy ground, his hands held at shoulder height. He watched for any lapse of attention from the other.

Nails asked, "Where's your horse?"

"Tied back there."

Nails unwrapped the reins from the hitchrail and stepped up quickly, seating himself in the saddle. The pistol never wavered. "Let's go get your horse."

Nodding, Ki turned and walked back through the fine mist. Obviously Nails was not going to shoot him here, in the settlement. They would go a few miles into the woods for that. The body might not be discovered for a year or more. Nails had not patted him down for a hideaway gun or a second knife; he apparently had much faith in his own ability with the six-gun.

And he evidently did not know about the *shuriken*. It was Ki's only hole card.

When they reached the horse, Nails took the reins and told him to mount. His gaze was steady; he was making no mistakes.

Nails indicated the path east, and Ki complied. Stealthily his fingers crept up and touched one of the throwing stars. Nails, behind him, said nothing.

Huge pine branches closed over their heads, and it was very dark. Ki considered turning in the saddle suddenly—but of course Nails would expect that and be ready for him. He must not do anything the other would expect.

They came out of the trees into a narrow plain with what was probably a dry wash in summer. Now it was a raging stream. They had probably come a mile from the settlement. A gunshot or two would not be heard from here.

Ki said, "Do you know what they found on the mountain?"

"Silver," Nails replied. "A huge vein of it."

"Yes, but not all. Silver is often found with gold. There was more gold than silver."

Nails was silent. Ki glanced around. The other was glaring at him. Nails said, "More gold than silver?"

"Twice as much." Would Nails believe that? The man's face showed his rage. He clicked the hammer on the pistol, back and forth. "Those goddamn Basques!"

"They'll all be very rich," Ki said softly, fingers creeping to his vest.

Nails lost his composure for a moment. He swore, glanced to the north toward the mountain—and Ki's fingers closed around a *shuriken* and hurled it.

It tore out Nails's throat. For a second his wild eyes stared at Ki—he fired the pistol with a last gasp—and fell from the saddle as the gray pranced.

The shot went into the sky and the pistol skittered away.

Ki leaned on the pommel, peering down at the body of his enemy. He sighed deeply. That had been a near thing. In another moment, he was positive, Nails would have shot him in the back.

He got down slowly, brought the gray back and heaved the body over the saddle.

It was a long trip back to Eagle Rock.